tuned in

EPISODE #3

true teamwork

by Julia DeVillers

Printed in the United States of America

First edition

ISBN 0-9678906-8-3

Visit www.limitedtoo.com

introduction

♡

OK, so **I LOVE** music, right? I've got my favorite singers! And my favorite music groups!

♡

I LOVE to listen to music.

♡

So how excited am I? Because I get to help plan a real music concert.

And not just any concert! Noooo, this is not just any ordinary concert. It's going to be a GIGANTIC, HUMONGOUS, TOTALLY COOL music festival with lots of famous singers and groups.

And the concert is for girls. ALL girls. Yup ... for Girls Only!

It's called Toopalooza. As in TOOpalooza. As in, like, Limited TOO. 'Cuz they're the ones setting up this awesome music festival.

The music festival I get to help plan.

Yup, right now I am supposed to listen to music by some new music groups. And pick which group I like best. And give my opinion to Limited Too on which group I (yes, me!) think should perform at the concert.

Is this a normal thing that happens to me? Am I some major music business person? Who gets to be like, hmmm, this song is pretty good. I like this group. They've got star potential. Yup, I like this group. Let's make them all stars!!

Oh, puh-lease. I'm just me! Regular Maddy Elizabeth Sparks!

I mean, only a couple weeks ago, nothing exciting had ever happened to me in my entire life! And then I went to the mall and got stuck in the bathroom with these three girls.

Kacey! Isabel! And Claire!

We were all total strangers. But now we're totally all friends!!

And then ... we sorta got "discovered" by these people from Limited Too. Who said we could help them with all this stuff so they'd know exactly what girls like. And then we got to be models on the cover of Limited Too's catazine! And we got to go to Hollywood and be on a TV show!!!

It was like completely out of nowhere.

These crazy, incredible, unbelievable things keep happening!

And now ...

WE GET TO HELP PLAN A MAJOR MUSIC FESTIVAL!

I get to help plan this concert ... Me! Maddy Elizabeth Sparks!

Soooo fun!

Sooooo cool!

This totally **ROCKS!**

I mean a couple days ago, I was just planning for the first day of school. And now ... I'm helping plan a huge concert!!!

How did THAT happen? OK, let me tell you the deal ....

chapter 1

This Journal Belongs to:

PRIVATE!   Maddy Elizabeth Sparks   KEEP OUT!!

Zack, STOP READING OR I'M TELLING!!!!

Q: What thing can totally make or break my life right now?

A: The letter in my hand. My class schedule for this year!!

When mom told me I had mail I was psyched! I love to get mail!

Maybe it was a letter from Taylor, my BFF who moved to California! It couldn't be an answer already to the fan letter I sent to Austin Hamilton ... or could it?

Austin Hamilton! He's a TV star on The Zoe Zone! A TV star I met in real and true life on my trip to Hollywood a couple weeks ago.

YES! HOLLYWOOD! I still can't believe I was in Hollywood! Hel-looo? Me in Hollywood? It was AWESOME!!! But now I'm back here at home. In Columbus, Ohio.

So anyway ... I had mail! And it was my class schedule for school. The classes I would be in -- in TWO days! Yes! School was starting in TWO days! YIKES!

And so ... in two days ... this would be my life:

Homeroom

1st	Math
2nd	Science
3rd	Lunch
4th	Social Studies
5th	Language Arts
6th	Spanish/Study Hall
7th	Choir/Wellness

Looked OK. Pretty normal. The usual math, science, ..

Except choir? I'm taking choir? Not that I don't love music. 'Cuz I SO do. It's just I love music when somebody ELSE is singing it!

Because when I sing? Ugh. I'm like this:

Croakkkkk! Waaaaaaaaaaak! ♩

So how did I get stuck in choir with MY voice? At least it's only every OTHER day. It switches with Wellness. Not that I'll be great at Wellness either. Because I'm thinking that means gym. And I'm not exactly sporty. Like how I tried out for cheerleading? I was SO not good enough. My jumps, cartwheels, and flips were, well, so ... not the best.

I didn't make the team.

All my friends made it. **ALL** of them. But I'm over it. I'm not SO bummed about it anymore. It's going to be a great school year even if I'm not a cheerleader! Maybe I'm not going to cheer on the football team! But I can cheer myself on ... to have an awesome school year!

Yay Maddy!

Gimme an M! A! D! D! Y! Gooooo, Maddy!

Maddy, Maddy, she's our man! If she can't do it, nobody can!

Or something like that.

YAY! Awesome school year!!!

G2g. Mom's calling. Phone's for me!

This is going to be the worst school year EVER. Ever in the HISTORY of school years.

Because it was Brittany on the phone. And she was sooooo excited to get the class schedules. And she was checking with everyone to see who was in her classes.

"So Maddy," she goes. "What did you get? What's your schedule?"

I told her. And she said ...

"Third period lunch, Maddy? You have third period lunch? Bummer! Because I have fifth period lunch. So we can't sit together. And it's not just me. Everybody else has fifth period, too. Because all the cheerleaders get lunch together so we can use it as practice if we want. So EVERYBODY has fifth period lunch! "

Everybody?

Brittany was still talking ...

"Yeah! Seriously, fifth period lunch is me, Haley, Danielle, Shana, Quinn, Caroline, Amanda ...."

Buzz ... my head was buzzing. This was SO not good. Because lunch is WAY important! I mean if you don't know anybody at lunch, who are you supposed to sit with?!!! Yourself??!

MYSELF???

Eek!

"Chelsea B, Surya, Maggie ... yup, everybody!" Brittany continued. "But the good news is I'm in your choir and wellness! So at least you have that with me! It's last period, so we can walk to the buses together, too. Except wait! No we can't. We'll be taking different buses because you'll be going straight home and I'll be staying after for cheerleading with everybody else."

AUGH!

Hey wait! I had an idea!

"Maybe I can get my schedule switched," I said to Brittany. "So I can be in lunch with you guys!"

"Oh, sorry Maddy. But that's not going to work," Brittany said. "I heard Jordan Cooper already tried it. You know Jordan? She didn't make cheerleading, like you? She used to think she was all that. Hah! She SO didn't make the team. Anyway, Jordan Cooper tried to switch, so she could be with Chelsea B. and Shana but ... no go. The school told her that they have enough girls in 5th Period Lunch already. I guess because all of the cheerleaders are in it! And that's a lot of girls! I mean, everybody! Me, Haley, Danielle, Amanda, Quinn, Caroline and Shana."

AUGH, AUGH, and ... AUGH!!!!!!!!!

So I was not going to have any of my friends in lunch. I was not going to have any of my friends on the bus ride home.

I had nobody to sit with in the cafeteria. I was going to be a **LUNCH LOSER!**

I had nobody to sit with on the bus. I was going to be a **BUS LOSER!**

This is going to be the worst school year of my LIFE!

"This is going to be the best school year of my life!" Brittany was going on. And on. And on. All cheerful and happy and la la la cheerleading la la la. "But OK, gotta go! The Cheerleader's Car Wash starts in an hour! Bye-eeeeee!"

Bye-eeee Brittany. Buh-bye. See you and all my friends like ... NEVER! Not at lunch! Not on the bus ride home!

AUGH!!!!!!

I stared at my schedule. It hadn't magically changed. Third period lunch. Third period lunch that started at 9:45. In the morning.

In the morning?!?!?!

Wait a minute. I have to eat lunch at 9:45 in the morning? No way, that's like breakfast time!!!

Aw, geez. AUGH!!!!!

chapter 2

So I'd be eating **brunch** alone at school this year. Way harsh.
Bad enough I was going to kind of a new school this year. They
put up a new building and were combining two schools. New
teachers! New bus! New lockers! And ... new other people.

So yeah, I'll still be going to school with Danielle and Haley
and Brittany. But all these other new people! And nobody to
sit with at lunch!!!

This was seriously depressing. Even my mood necklace was
the brownish color. That meant super bummed out! I picked
up my guinea pig, Sugar. I cranked up my radio. And flopped
on my bed. I was ready to tune out the world.

Yup. I was ready to do some major bumming.

I flipped through the stations to find the right song. I wanted
a really, really sad song. To match my mood. Oh perfect, here's
that new Skyler Hope song.

What will I do? I'm so lost without you!
Life is so dark, so tired, so blue ....

I listened to Skyler Hope sing all sad. Feeling all sad and lonely
with me. I know how you feel, Skyler. Life stinks.

Song over. I shifted Sugar so I could reach for the dial to find a new sad, sad song.

"And now for the debut song from a new local group ..." the deejay was saying.

Think you're facing ... the world all alone?
It's all going by without you ....

Hm. I flopped back on my bed. Good. This song was pretty sad sounding.

Think that things will never be good again?

Yeah, that's what I was thinking. Sing it, new local group whoever you are.

You think you're alone, girl?
Just listen to this song, girl!
And see that's all so wrong, girl ... 'cuz ...

Things are looking up! Oh yeah!
Things are LOOKING UP!

Today is my day, to change how I feel.
It is time for me to see, exactly what is real.

Hey! They tricked me! It was turning into a fast song! A happy song! I thought it was going to be a sad song. For my baaad mood.

Happiness comes, and happiness goes.
But today is the day, my happiness grows.

OK, but hm. I wasn't even changing the dial. This song was pretty catchy.

'Cuz ... things are LOOKING UP! Yeah, things are looking up!

Prrrrp! Prrrrp! Sugar was making that happy guinea pig noise.

"You like this song, too, Sugar?" I asked her.

I picked up the microphone that came with my CD player. I put Sugar back in her cage. I got on my bed. I faced the mirror.

I jumped off the bed and locked the door. I learned my lesson from watching TV and movies. You know, the little brother is always sneaking over and spying on their big sister while she's lip synching. And taking videos or pictures of it or something.

And the sister gets totally embarrassed.

And I've got one of THOSE little brothers. So I was taking nooooo chances, thank you very much. Door was LOCKED.

I started lip synching into the microphone.

Happiness comes, and happiness goes.
But today is the day, my happiness grows.

I was movin. I was jumpin. I was dancing around my bed!

Things are LOOKING UP! Yeah, things are looking up!

Yes! OK! I can go to school and face the world alone! Because ...

It won't be for long, girl!
Just think about this song, girl!
THINGS ARE LOOKING UP! Yeah ...
Things couldn't be looking any better!

YEAH!

Whew! Song over!

Wow! That was a seriously good song! Hey! My mood necklace is blue-green! That means, pretty happy! Not so bummed anymore! I flopped down on my bed. But you know what? I didn't feel like flopping out anymore. Yup! I felt much better now!

"Didja like that song as much as I did?" the deejay asked. "Now it's time for a weather check with Buzz in our traffic copter ...."

Bummer, I missed the name of the song. And the group. I wonder who it was. Hope I hear it again sometime!

JIGGLE! JIGGLE!

My doorknob started shaking. JIGGLE! JIGGLE! PUSH!

Zack! Trying to come into my room.

"Ha, ha, Zack!" I called out. "Door's locked! You can't come in!"

When you have Zack as your brother you better remember to lock your door. You never know what will happen.

"OK! I'll leave. Guess I'll tell her your answer is no!" I heard Zack say.

"Answer to what?" I asked him, suspiciously. "Guess you'll tell who my answer is no."

"Oh, nothing," he said.

WHAT?!!!

"I'll tell you if you pay me two bucks," Zack said.

"Tell me, Zack," I warned.

"One dollar," Zack said.

"MOOOOOOOM!" I yelled. "Zack's bribing me!!!!!"

"OK, OK," he whined. "Our new neighbor down the street asked me to ask you if you want to dogsit for her when she is on vacation?"

Dogsit? Me?

Um, yes! Yes! I love dogs! I mean I really, really LOVE dogs!

Soft fur! Wet noses! The way they snuggle up with you! The way they are your very best friend!

I LOVE DOGS!

And I SO want one.

Ask me if I have a dog! Noooo.

Number of times I have asked dad if we can get a dog:

★ One bajillion.

Number of times dad has said NO:

★ One bajillion.

"NO DOGS IN OUR HOUSE, Maddy!" he says.

Last time I asked, he said "I just know that I would end up having to feed it. I would end up having to walk it. I would end up having to pick up dog poo. Too messy. Too needy. Too much trouble."

"But I can do it, dad!" I told him. Promised him! Begged him!

"I just don't think you're ready for the responsibility of a dog," dad said.

But now ... this is soooo perfect! I can dogsit! I can show dad that I can take care of a dog! I can prove to him that Maddy Elizabeth Sparks **IS** ready for a dog. I will be the BEST dogsitter ever!

I opened my door. Raced past Zack! Yeeeeeessss! Dogsitting!

Would mom and dad let me do it? Would they say yes?

I ran into the family room where dad was. What could he say? What would dad say?

a) I don't think so, Maddy, that's a big responsibility.
b) Sorry, Maddy. I don't think you're quite ready yet.
c) No, Maddy. Just NO.

What dad DID say?

d) NONE of the above.

He did say ... "I spoke to Miss Phipp. I told her you would stop down and talk to her about watching her dog. Your mom and I agreed that yes, Maddy, you may dogsit."

YE-EEEEEEE-SSSS!

"Thanks, dad!" I said.

And bolted before he could change his mind!

Out the door ... down the street ... to the new neighbor's house!

Miss Phipp. She'd only just moved in a couple of weeks ago! I didn't even know what kind of dog it was! Was it a big huge hairy dog? A cute wittle foo-foo dog? A fuzzy little puppy?

Maddy's Ultimate Dog Wish List:

     a) Golden Retrievers
     b) Pugs
     c) Poodles
     d) Newfoundlands
     e) Little weiner dogs

But it really doesn't matter! I love ALL dogs! I can't wait to meet this dog!!!

This Journal Belongs to:

Maddy Elizabeth Sparks
_____

I AM AN OFFICIAL DOGSITTER!

The doggie's name is Scrumptious!!! She is a little foofy dog with long white fur! She's so bouncy! So fluffy! So happy! She's just soooo cute!

Miss Phipp says she's NEVER left Scrumptious before.

Dogsitting "To Do" list:

1. Feed Scrumptious.

2. Walk Scrumptious. (And don't forget a special doggie treat if she does her business!)

3. Make sure Scrumptious stays happy!

I'M GONNA BE THE BEST DOGSITTER EVER!!

chapter 3

From: BrittanyCheer
Send to: Haleygrl
CC: Dani55, Shanastar, MaggieMegs, Jadarox, ChelCB,
CareBear143, QuinnQT, Maddyblue
Subject: Cheerleading Scoopage

Girlies! Only 2 days til school! First Day Sitch:

1. Guess what! We're going to wear our uniforms
the first day! Coach (my mom) said so we show
school unity and pride in our new school!
2. We're going to all pack lunch. Pack not buy. I
will get there early to scope out the BEST lunch
table.
3. Practice starts right after 7th period. Late
bus, cheerleaders!

From: BrittanyCheer
Send to: Maddyblue
CC: Dani55, Shanastar, MaggieMegs, Jadarox,
ChelCB, CareBear143, QuinnQT, Haleygrl
Subject: Oops!

Sorry Maddy! I didn't mean to cc you!

OK. She has to STOP doing that. Is Brittany doing that on purpose
or WHAT? That's the thing about Brittany. It's hard to tell if
she's being mean or just ... a total ditz!

Either way. That email put me right back in that bad mood.

AUGH!!!!

But, I can't even think about that now. Because right now I had a job to do. As a professional working person. I was about to start dogsitting!

Today was my first day of dogsitting!

And I just knew seeing cute little poochie Scrumptious would cheer me up!!!!

I went over to Miss Phipp's house. I unlocked the door.

"Here I am, Scrumptious! Your favorite dogsitter is here!"

I waited for Scrumptious to bounce out and give me more licks! Where is that sweet little dog?!!!

"I'm here Scrumptious!" I called. Mwah! Mwah! Little kissy noises! Come on Scrumptious! I checked her little pink satin dog bed. No Scrumptious. I checked the couch. No Scrumptious. And then I found her.

Under a chair. Just lying there.

"Scrumptious?" I asked. Was she asleep?

Nope. Because she opened one eye. And shut it. She sighed. She just lay there, totally a flop.

"Want some food?" I asked her. "Yummy, yummy doggie dinner!"

Dogsitting To Do List:
1. Feed Scrumptious

I brought out her dog dish. I filled it up with brown chunks of smelly dog stuff.

She wasn't interested.

"Want your squeaky toy, Scrumptious?" Squeeeeeeeeeeeeel! I squeezed it. I shook it in front of her face.

Scrumptious just opened one eye. And went, SIGHHHHHHH.

I tried giving her a treat although she hadn't done her business.

"OK, don't tell Miss Phipp. But here's a little treat for you!"

Scrumptious looked at the treat. And closed her eyes again. She put her chin on her paws. And just laid there. Making sad breathing noises like SIGHHHHHHHHHHHHH.

Scrumptious was seriously sad.

I got down on the floor. And stuck my head under the chair.

Scrumptious opened her eyes. And looked at me. Like, I am a sad, sad dog, Maddy. I am just soooo, sooooo sad.

On a scale of sadness, she was like ....

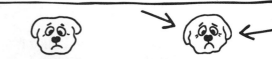

a little bummed   very sad   major depressed!!!

"OH, you poor little baby," I said. "You're so sad. Maybe some lovies will make you feel better."

I laid my head next to hers. I petted her fur.

But Scrumptious just lay there, with her chin on her paws. Her eyes closed. Going SIGHH. So, so sad. I felt so bad for her. What could I do? Miss Phipp wouldn't be home for FOUR DAYS!

Dogsitting To Do List:
2. Walk Scrumptious. She gets a treat if she does her business!

OK, I should at least try to walk her. I picked her up. She just flopped in my arms. I carried her out the door to the front yard. I put on her leash.

"Come on, Scrumptious," I said. "A nice little walk! Exercise is supposed to cheer you up!"

Nothing. I tugged on the leash a little.

"A little walky! Let's go for a little walky!"

She didn't move her legs. So I ended up kinda dragging her. OK, this was definitely not working.

But then, Scrumptious piddled! She did do her business!

"Yay, Scrumptious!" I said. "You get a doggie treat! Yummy!"

I pulled a treat out of my pocket! That should cheer her up, right?

Scrumptious sniffed at the treat. She flopped down on the sidewalk. And closed her eyes ... AGAIN!

Oh! She was still SOOOO sad! Bummer!

POOR DOGGIE. Scrumptious opened one eye and looked at me. Like she was saying, Maddy! Please help me! I am so sad!

I lay down on my stomach on the lawn so my face was close to hers. Scrumptious opened one eye and looked at me.

"Poor, poor little Scrumptious," I said to her. What can I do to cheer you up?

I kissed her little nose. She just sighed. I petted her long white fur. She just shlumped. I made a silly face at her. She did open both her eyes.

OK! Maybe I was getting somewhere. I made another silly face. She blinked at me. But at least she was looking at me! I tried to make her laugh.

Um, do dogs laugh?

I started to act like a dog. I got on all fours. I stuck out my tongue and went Pant! Pant! I made doggie noises. Rrrrr, rrrr! Rrowf! Rrowf!

I rolled over and played dead. I lay on my back and stuck my hands and legs up in the air. Be happy, Scrumptious!

"Look at me, Scrumptious!" I told her. "Crazy Maddy! Come on, girl! Isn't this funny?"

Well, she had picked her head up. Was looking at least a little interested. Maybe she had a sense of doggie humor!

Or maybe she just thought I was crazy.

I lay there on my back and waved my arms and legs around.

I rolled around on the ground. I barked. I whined.

"That's right, Scrumptious! Look at crazy Maddy doggy! I'm a silly doggy! Funny! Funny!" I said.

Then I heard laughing. Like a seriously loud HA, HA, HA!

Oh no! I looked up. Oh great. Just GREAT!!

My brother Zack. Laughing and pointing at me.

Laughing really hard. Falling off his bike laughing so hard.

"My sister has LOST it!" he gasped. "Freaking out on the ground! Talking to a dog!"

Oh, ha, ha Zack. Soooo funny. I'm trying to cheer up this dog, OK? Ha, ha.

Red-face Rating: ★★★ out of ☆★★★☆ stars.
Now I know where some of my dogsitting money is going. To pay Zack not to tell anybody else about this. ARGH!!!!

I looked at Scrumptious. She was all flopped out again. With her chin on her paws. She had closed her eyes again.

Oh NO! I really thought I was cheering her up. And now ... sad dog!

"Go away, Zack," I yelled. "You are **SO** not helping."

"Mom told me to tell you that you have to come home!" Zack said. "Ha, ha! I'm sooooo glad I came over to see this!"

He cracked up again.

Go away, Zack. Go far, far away.

I picked up Scrumptious and carried her back in the house. I put her in her little pink satin dog bed. She sighed, laid her head down, and closed her eyes.

I'm so sorry, Scrumptious. But I have to go home.

I waved good-bye. She didn't even look at me. I locked the door. And walked back to my house.

A total and complete FAILURE.

I AM THE WORST DOGSITTER EVER.

Because remember what I was supposed to do?

Dogsitting To Do List:
3. Make sure Scrumptious stays happy!

I totally blew it! Scrumptious was sooooooo not happy!

Scrumptious must feel so sad without Miss Phipp. She must be so lonely! Her best friend in the world had left her. It must seem like everyone in the world has left her!!!

I knew that feeling. First Taylor moves to California. Taylor! My very best BFF in the universe! Had to move a gajillion miles away!!!! Then the whole "being left out of lunch and the bus and the cheerleading team" thing ....

Scrumptious, I know how you feel.

Sad and bummed out and all ALONE!

I walked in my front door. My dad was in the kitchen on the phone. "Hi sweetie, how did dogsitting go?"

TERRIBLE! AWFUL! I am the **WORST DOGSITTER** ever!!!

Oh, can't let dad know that. 'Cuz I want to show him I can do it! I have to be the best *Taking Care of Dog Person* ever! So maybe, just maybe he will let ME get a dog!

Uh ... um ....

"Uh! Um ..." I started to say ...

Rrrrrrrrrrring!!!!

Telephone!

Whew! Saved by the bell!

"Maddy, it's for you," dad held out the phone to me. "It's Lauren from Limited Too."

Lauren! From Limited Too Headquarters! Lauren was the one who first got me and Isabel, Kacey, and Claire to be the Too Crew! I was always psyched to talk to her!

And I still always felt ... surprised when she called. Like, huh? They're calling ME? Me, plain old Maddy Elizabeth Sparks. Sometimes I just stop and think ... I CAN'T BELIEVE I'M PART OF THE TOO CREW!

I mean, it's crazy! One day I'm in a realllllly bad mood and then all of a sudden ... something amazing happens!!!!

"Hi Lauren!" I said into the phone.

"Maddy! We've got your next assignment for you," Lauren said. "Do you like music?"

Do I like music?

I have posters on my wall of my fave music groups!

I have pins of my fave groups all over my backpack!

I was planning to buy a new CD with my dogsitting money!

Yes! YES! And **YES**!!!

"YES!" I told Lauren.

"Great," she said. "Because Limited Too is going to host a music fest. It's going to be called Toopalooza.We'd like to have the TOO Crew help us out with some of the planning. We'll ask you some questions about what you'd like to see. And have you help us learn what other girls would like, as well. We'll all meet at Headquarters tomorrow to have a brainstorming session."

Cool!

And then, WAY cool. Get this. Lauren told me who would be at Toopalooza:

- ★ Aaron Carter!
- ★ Ashlee Simpson!
- ★ Jessica Simpson!
- ★ Mandy Moore!
- ★ Play!
- ★ Nick Cannon!

And more!

Ohmigosh!

And some new singers will be singing there, too! They'll get to play a major concert for the very first time! And we will get to help pick them!

How cool is that!

Way cool!

I am SO there!!!

chapter 4

I entered the Limited Too headquarters building with my mom.
Oh, and Zack, too. I was psyched to be there. But nervous! I hoped
I could do a good job here since my other job was ... well ...
not going very good.

Dogsitting Day #2 was no better than Dogsitting Day #1. It was
actually worse! Because Scrumptious just lay there. Again. All
lumpy and shlumpy! No matter what I did! She didn't eat her
food, or her treats, or anything! That was one depressed dog!!!!

Anyway ... I'm going to forget about that—for now.

We walked into the building. I got buzzed in. I went over to the
big desk up front to check in.

"Hi!" I said to the woman at the front desk with the brown
hair.

"Hi Maddy!" she said, giving me a visitor's badge. "I'll buzz
Lauren and let her know you're here."

Cool! She knew my name! Some people kinda knew me here! I
felt a little famous! Hee!

I stuck my visitor's badge to my shirt. I was wearing a red, short sleeve shirt and denim skirt. I was wearing my mood necklace, too. It was bluish-greenish. Pretty happy! Maybe a little nervous!

"Pssst, hey Maddy!" Zack whispered. "Guess who I am?"

Zack lay down on the floor and ... OH NO! Zack! NOT HERE!

"Woof! Woof!" Zack was rolling around on the floor. Acting like a dog. Pretending to play dead. And barking. "Woof! Woof!"

"Get it, Maddy?" Zack said. "Get it? I'm like you acting like a dog on Miss Phipp's front lawn!"

"MOOOOOOOOOM!" I hissed to my mother. "Make him stop! Before somebody sees him!"

Oh no! Lauren was coming!

"I see you brought your dog with you today, Maddy" Lauren said, smiling.

Red-face Rating: ★★★☆ out of ☆★★★☆ stars.
Somebody saw him! But I guess it could be worse, he could be telling people WHY he was doing that ...

"Want to know why I was acting all like a freaking-out dog," Zack was telling Lauren. "It's because Maddy was at our neighbor's house and she was –"

I shot a look at my mom! STOP HIM!

Mom went over and covered his mouth with her hand. She said hi to Lauren, waved good-bye to me and totally dragged Zack out of the building.

WHEW, thanks mom! Mom saves the day!!!! I peeked over at Lauren to see if she thought I was total weirdo.

"Don't worry, Maddy," Lauren said. "I had two little brothers. TWINS! I went through it, too."

Lauren always knew the right thing to say! I felt better now.

"The TOO Crew is waiting for you in the conference room," she told me. "I'll take you there."

We walked into the room. And there was Kacey! And Isabel!! And Claire!!! The entire TOO Crew was here!!!!

"MADDY!" Kacey, Isabel, and Claire said. All happy to see me! They were sitting together on one end of a long table. I went and gave everyone a hug. I was soooo happy to see them!

"Nice necklace," Isabel whispered to me. She had on a mood necklace, too! Ours were both bright blue!

Bright blue meaning super happy! 'Cuz I was super happy to see the TOO Crew!!!!

"Look what Lauren gave us!" Kacey said, wiggling around in her chair and waving something. "It's a postcard from Jennifer!"

Jennifer! The Grand Prize Winner of the Zoe Zone Contest. She was way sweet. Really shy and nervous, and then she ended up being our friend!

Kacey read the postcard out loud.

Dear Maddy and Kacey and Isabel and Claire,

I'm back in Arizona! School started already and guess what? I made the basketball team! And I have a new friend. Her name is Ava and she loves the Zoe Zone too. I can't wait to see us all on TV.

Luv,
Jennifer

Awwww, that was so nice!

"Wait, there's a PS," Kacey said.

P.S. Maddy! We went to the zoo here. And I saw a monkey. And I thought of you!

Awww ... HEY! Wait a minute!

"Monkey Girl!" Isabel teased me. That was a joke from our trip to Hollywood. It's sort of a long story, but I had acted like a monkey to make Jennifer relax. Kinda embarrassing. But kinda nice she was thinking of me. Even if it's as a monkey.

"Your episode of The Zoe Zone will be aired in a few months," Lauren said. WOO HOO! I couldn't wait to see us all on TV!!!!

"We'll get started soon," Lauren said. "But we are going to have a few more girls joining us today. They should be here any minute."

Some man came in and told Lauren the other girls were waiting out front. She said she'd be right back.

"I'm so excited! I mean, how cool does this music fest sound?" Kacey asked. She was bouncing all over her seat. As usual, it was hard for her to sit still! She was as bouncy as the volleyball picture on her t-shirt!

"So cool!" Isabel said. She had pulled her long, dark hair into a ponytail. She was wearing a dark red tank, jeans and platforms. And a mood necklace just like me! And it was bright blue, too!

"I wonder who the other girls are who are coming," said Claire. She was wearing her blond hair straight and was wearing a short sleeve shirt, a flowered skirt and sandals. We were about to find out. In through the door walked ... Oh! No!

PIPER and SIERRA.

Piper, one of the models from the catazine shoot. Piper, who was all "I should be on the cover of the catazine because I am a professional model. I am in TV commercials. And you guys are a bunch of NOBODY's."

That's what she was like.

And her friend Sierra.

OK, Piper was just **So Not Nice.** And Sierra wasn't much better.

But maybe, just maybe, they'd gotten better?

"OH," Piper said, looking around at us. "You guys are doing this, too? My agent told me this was a professional job."

"Maybe this is the wrong room," Sierra suggested.

Guess they hadn't gotten better!

Then they sat down at the other end of the table.

"Hello," Claire tried asking them politely. "Are you excited to be helping plan the music fest?" Piper and Sierra ignored her. Kacey shot me a look, like Hel-lo? Who do they think they are?!

"Excuse me. Claire asked you if you are excited to help plan the music fest," Isabel said loudly in a Don't-Mess-With-Me-Voice!

Piper rolled her eyes.

"It's not that big a deal ... for ME. My father knows tons of people in the music biz. So I get to do these kinds of things all the time," Piper said, all braggy-like.

"Yeah, all the time!" Sierra said.

Ooooooookay then. Kacey shot me another look like, UGH! But Isabel was kinda smiling. I think she thought they were kind of funny. Isabel was really good at dealing with rude people! She mostly just ignored them!

I had a hard time doing that. I always felt like I was doing something wrong! Or I felt stupid! Or embarrassed!

Lauren walked in the room. "We have one more girl joining us," she said. "This is her first time here."

"MORE amateurs," Piper whispered. "Jeesh!"

And in walked the other girl. And it was ...

chapter 5

BRITTANY?!!!!

Brittany was here at Limited Too Headquarters?

My FRIEND Brittany??!!!

"Brittany?!" I said. "What are you doing here!"

I mean, Brittany was always kind of jealous that I got to do TOO Crew stuff. She actually told me that once. Well, so now she gets to do some of it, too? I guess that's cool. OK, I could be happy for her. Except ... weeeeelll ...

I kind of liked having TOO Crew separate from my school friends, you know?

Plus, Brittany was ... um ... you know ... kinda hard to deal with sometimes!

"Hiiiiiiiiii, Maddy!" Brittany said in this super sweet fakey voice. She came over and gave me a big hug. She scoped out the room.

"Hiiiiii, everybody," she said. She looked at me, like introduce me!

"This is Brittany," I said to everyone else. "She's my friend from school. Um, this is a surprise!"

"I know!" Brittany giggled. "Isn't this so great, Maddy? Now I get to do all this, too? Remember that talent agency you told me about? That I should sign up for? Well, they took me right away! And this is my first job!"

"ANOTHER amateur," Piper snorted.

Brittany looked at Piper. "Oh! I know who you are! You're the Taco Tiko Princess. The agency told me about you. They said you're one of their best models!"

"Well," Piper said. "THAT'S true."

"And ohmigosh, I just love your hair!" Brittany squealed. "Did you go to Joseph? That looks SO Joseph. I'm just dying to have my hair done just like that!"

"Well, yes," Piper patted her long, streaky blond hair. "I did."

"Sooo great," Brittany said.

GAG.

"Pssst, Maddy!" Isabel whispered to me. "Is that ...?"

I nodded. Yes, it was THE Brittany. Isabel knew that Brittany was stressing me out! At cheerleading tryouts! At home! Even in Hollywood! I told her Brittany was going to try to be better. And I would try staying friends with her. See if it was worth it.

But um, well ... today wasn't helping much. Isabel gave me a sympathetic look. Like, oh, poor Maddy. Having to deal with THAT!

"So you're friends with that girl?" Sierra asked Brittany, waving over at me. Sierra moved her chair closer to Piper's.

"Oh, Maddy and I have known each other since we were like infants," Brittany answered. "Like our moms were friends and stuff. So Piper, while you're here, maybe I can ask you some questions about your successful modeling career?"

Piper patted the chair next to her. Brittany sat down.

Brittany and Piper started chatting. Like "Ooh! Piper, the way you said 'Mmm burritos' was so perfect!" "Yes, it was, wasn't it?" Blah, blah, blah.

GAG!!!!! BARF!!!! PUKE!!!!

Brittany + Piper = UGH!!!!!!

Sierra didn't look too happy about it. Neither did I!

Lauren came back in the room. Everyone stopped talking.

"Have you all had a chance to introduce yourselves?" she asked. We nodded. "Great. Then let's get started."

Lauren tuned us in on the whole Toopalooza event:

- ☆ There will be some really cool booths with fun games, contests and stuff.
- ☆ Some REALLY famous groups and singers are gonna be performing there!
- ☆ One new group, *TOO's U-Pick Challenge* winner, will also perform ... and that's were we come in. WE are gonna help them pick the winner!

COOL!

Lauren explained. "We surveyed many, many girls and they voted on their top four choices. But the choices are so close, we thought you girls could narrow it down to one.

I'll put in some DVDs of the groups for you to watch. I'll give you girls an hour. Choose which group is your absolute favorite. And they will get to be the *TOO's U-Pick Challenge* winner!"

WOW!

She passed out some pieces of paper and pens. Stuck a DVD into a TV in the corner. And said she would be back. In one hour!!!

"I probably already know these groups," Piper said. "My father gets me all the stuff before it comes out. He has a lot of connections."

"Ooooh, cool!" Brittany squealed.

"Yes! It's soooo cool!" Sierra squealed, too.

Kacey and I looked at each other, like Oh Puh-lease!

"Let's start the DVD," Isabel said. "Let's just watch and see what we think."

Kacey jumped up and turned off the lights. Isabel turned on the DVD. We watched as words flashed on the screen.

Candidates for *TOO's U-Pick Challenge!*

Group 1 was named The Feathers.

"Hi!" the guy on the video said. "We're the Feathers. We've been playing together for two years now. We like to ROCK!"

A group of two girls and two guys came on the screen. They were singing, rocking out on a stage. They were wearing mostly black pants and shirts. There were clips of them doing a couple different songs. They were good!

Group 2 was a singer named Nina Miles.

"Hi!" the girl on the video said. "I'm Nina Miles. I love to sing. I won a talent contest last year and now I just came out with my first video!"

Nina was pretty! She was a good singer. She sang a really bouncy song. She danced all over the place. She had brown wavy hair and wore a tank top, jeans, and tall boots. I felt like dancing along with her. I liked her!

Group 3 was a group named POSE.

"We're POSE," a girl on the video said. "The group with attitude. Serious attitude. I'm Love. The lead singer. I'm named Love 'cuz everyone luuuuuuvs everything about me. So you ready? We're going to show you how awesome we are!"

Three girls sang and danced. They were pretty. Really pretty. They wore tube tops, really sparkly silver pants, and spiky heels. They were really good dancers. But, well. They just had these looks on their faces. Like not smiling. And being like, well, really stuck-up looking.

So, I guess they were good. But I didn't like them that much.

Group 4 was a group named INSPIRE.

"Hi!" four girls on the video said. "We're Eden! And Morgan! And Alexa! And Sabrina! We're INSPIRE! We hope to inspire you with our song, *Looking Up!*"

They were sweet and smiley. They were wearing more regular clothes than POSE. Like not all sparkly, but still really cool. One girl was on the guitar and one was at the piano.

And then the music started. The singers started singing.

Thinking you're facing ... the world all alone?
Thinking they're all leaving without you?

Hey. Ohmigosh!

You think you're alone, girl?
Just listen to this song, girl!
And see that's all so wrong, girl,
'cuz it won't be long girl ... 'cuz ....

HEY! That's the song! The song that was on the radio! When I was so bummed out about lunch and the bus and school and ...

THAT'S THE SONG THAT TOTALLY CHEERED ME UP!!!

Things are looking up!
Yeah! Things are looking up!
Today is my day to change how I feel,
It's time for me to see exactly what is real.

OK, can I just say this. I LOVE that song! And INSPIRE was soooo cool! They were really cute! Sometimes they were singing and dancing. And the video showed clips of them all playing instruments, too. Like one was on piano, one on guitar, one on drums. And one even picked up a flute and did a little solo thing.

Happiness comes, and happiness goes.
But today is the day, my happiness grows.
Things are LOOKING UP! Yeah!
Things couldn't be looking any better!

"Thanks for watching INSPIRE!" they all said.

And ... it was over! The tape was done. Kacey jumped up and turned off the TV.

"OK, why don't we all go around the table. And take turns saying who we want to vote for," Isabel said.

"Well, I'm thinking it's pretty obvious who should win," said Piper. "So why don't I go first and just save us all the effort. The best one was POSE. They were totally hot. Did you see Love? She was major gorgeous. And how cool is her name, Love."

"Yeah! That's what I was thinking, too!" Sierra said.

"Piper is totally right," Brittany agreed.

Piper was sitting there looking all like, yup ... end of discussion.

But huh! That was so not what I was thinking. Hm. I guess I was totally wrong? I had it totally the opposite way. I was thinking:

★ INSPIRE
★ Nina Miles
★ The Feathers
★ POSE

"OK, three for POSE," said Isabel. "Let's see what everybody else thought. Maddy, who did you like?"

"Um." Ugh. Why did I have to go next. I mean everyone so far voted for POSE. It would have been so easy to say, Yeah! Me too! Sure! I like POSE!

Especially with Brittany looking at me like that. Like that's what she expected me to say! I mean, what do I know about this stuff?

"Maddy, who did you really like best," Isabel asked. She looked at me like she expected me to say something else! So OK, I would!

"Uh, I actually liked INSPIRE best." I said in a squeaky voice.

"What did you like about them?" Isabel went on.

"I thought they were, um, way sweet and sounded soooo good. And they played their own instruments which is way cool."

"Oh, gimme a break," said Piper. "Instruments like the flute? I mean, REALLY!"

"Excuse me for interrupting," Claire said politely. "But I've taken flute. And what that girl was playing was really difficult. She was very talented."

"Maddy, anything else about INSPIRE you liked?" Isabel asked.

"Yeah," I said. "Um, what was so weird was I heard that song a couple of days ago? I was feeling really bummed out about this phone call I'd gotten. (I couldn't look at Brittany!) And *Looking Up* came on the radio. And it totally, well, made me feel better! I mean, it really did! I could totally relate to the song!"

Now I was on a roll. I stood up and kept going.

"And isn't that what they said?" I continued. "They want to inspire girls and I felt like, inspired when I listened to them. And isn't that something music is supposed to do?!!! So I vote for INSPIRE!!!!"

Whew! OK, then. I sat down.

Isabel smiled at me. "OK. 3 votes for POSE, 1 for INSPIRE."

"Claire?" Isabel asked.

"I liked INSPIRE, too. I thought they were really talented," she said. "And they seemed nice."

"I'm with INSPIRE, too," Isabel said. "Love the songs, love their voices. And they seemed so ... real. So 3 for POSE, 3 for INSPIRE. It's now a tie."

We all looked at Kacey. It was up to her! POSE? Or INSPIRE?

"Oh no!" Kacey laughed. "I hate to do this! But I was liking Nina Miles. She was so fun and full of energy and ..."

I could see that! Nina Miles was super bouncy! Like Kacey!!!!

"... she was my favorite," Kacey went on. "But I liked INSPIRE second best. So I guess I could vote for them, too!"

"No way!" Piper said. "That would be way unfair. It's 3 for POSE and 3 for INSPIRE and 1 for Nina Miles."

"So NOW what are we supposed to do?" Sierra whined.

"Well, I hate to say this but," Piper said in this super-sticky voice. "I really do know what I'm talking about. I'm kind of an expert in this area. I was actually in a music video."

"You WERE?!" Brittany gasped. "In a video!!?"
"For the Wanna Be's! You know, the rock group that sings *Get Off My Case, Get Out of My Face*?" Piper said. "I was Girl #3 in a video for another one of their songs. It was just a demo but I'm sure it will be out on music television really soon. Any day."

"That is SO COOL!" Brittany said. Piper smiled at her.

"Yeah!" said Sierra! "So cool, Piper!"

UCH! BLUCH!

"And I say we should pick POSE!" Piper the Music Expert said.

"Well, not so fast," Isabel said. She looked at Piper. Piper looked at Isabel.

Um ....

"OK, girls!" The door opened. Whew, Lauren was here!

"Who will be *TOO's U-Pick Challenge* winner?" Lauren asked us. "This is a very important decision! This will be a huge break for one of these singers or groups! So, who will it be?"

chapter 6

At the exact same time, Piper said "POSE!" and Isabel said, "We had a tie!"

Lauren looked at them. "Piper?" she asked.

"Well, we thought POSE was a no brainer. Like they are SO hot, WAY the best. But *they* mostly wanted that INSPIRE group," said Piper.

"I liked Nina Miles the best!" Kacey said, bouncing out of her seat. "So I couldn't break the tie! But INSPIRE was really my second choice! I almost would have voted for them!"

"But I really, really liked INSPIRE," I burst out. I couldn't help it! "I think they would be so great for girls to hear. I love their music, and I just LOVE their group!"

"Hm," Lauren said. "Let me check on something." She picked up her phone and asked to be connected to John. I had met John! He was the Limited Too guy who first asked us to be part of the TOO Crew!!! I think he was Lauren's boss or something. Lauren was talking to him on the phone.

"All right," Lauren said to all of us. "I can tell you feel passionate about your choices. I like that. Since we kind of have a tie, I'd like to go one step further. We'll have a little friendly competition. There will be two teams.

Team 1 is Piper, Brittany, and Sierra from the talent agency. Kacey, since you also liked INSPIRE, why don't you join the rest of the TOO Crew for Team 2."

"But that's not fair," Sierra pouted. "They have four and we have three!"

"Who cares," Piper said, tossing her hair. "We can win anyway."

"Moving on," said Lauren. "Each team will have a couple days to put together a presentation. Both teams will present at a local mall to an audience of girls. The presentation should help the audience decide which group they like better. Then the audience will vote on which group will be the *TOO's U-Pick Challenge* winner.

We'll call it *TOO's U-Pick Challenge* Contest! Whew, that's a mouthful," said Lauren.

OK, I got it. So:

- ☆ Team 1 would try to convince the audience that POSE should win.
- ☆ Team 2 (US!!!!) would try to convince the audience INSPIRE should win!

"Why don't you girls take a few minutes and get together with your team and create a game plan," Lauren said. "And I'll go see if your parents and guardians are here, yet."

A COMPETITION!!!!! YIKES!!!!!!

"This is so a no brainer!" Piper said, flipping her hair.

"Yeah, we can totally win this," Brittany agreed, flipping her hair, too.

"You guys have no chance!" Sierra said. "Alexa has no chance at all!"

Alexa? Who's Alexa?

"Who's Alexa?" Brittany asked. "I'm confused."

I saw Piper shoot Sierra a look. And wait a minute ... I just thought of something.

"Alexa!" I said. I ran over to the picture of the group INSPIRE. Hey! I recognized one of the singers in the group. It was a girl named Alexa. She'd been the other catazine model with us!!!!

"Ohmigosh!" Claire said. "I remember Alexa! She's in INSPIRE?! I didn't recognize her!"

Me neither! She had her hair all up and stuff! Plus I never expected somebody who lived around here to be in one of the groups!!!!

Cool!!!!

"Yeah! Alexa was sooo nice!" Kacey said. She looked at me. I knew what she was thinking. Alexa had been so nice to us at the catazine shoot. Unlike ...

Piper and Sierra!

"Yes, that's her," Piper said. "Alexa in INSPIRE lives here in Columbus. And she's represented by the same talent agency that me, Sierra, and Brittany are. They DO represent only the most talented performers. That's true."

"Yeah! We totally know Alexa!" Sierra said. "We saw her like two weeks ago when me and Piper tried out for this commercial. And Alexa got the job instead ..."

"OK, that's ENOUGH, Sierra," Piper said. "All that doesn't matter. POSE is still much better."

Hm.

"And POSE will win!" Brittany said. "Go POSE!" She got up and did a little cheer move. "I'm co-captain of the cheerleaders," she said to Piper.

Puh-lease. Wonder if I should let her know Isabel and Kacey were both captains of their cheerleading squads?

"OK, Crew! Let's get our plan together," Isabel said to me, Kacey, and Claire. We moved to the other corner of the room.

"Come on Talent Girls!" Piper said. "We're going to call ourselves the Talent Girls!"

"'Cuz we're from the talent agency!" said Sierra.

"And we're soooo talented, like POSE," Brittany said. She and Piper high-fived. Brittany looked at us. "No spying on our ideas!"

They went to the other side of the room, giggling.

Oh, hee hee.

OK, is it just me or do we really, really need to win this?

For INSPIRE! For Alexa! And because, OK, this is totally selfish but it's true! I don't want Piper, Brittany and Sierra to win!!!!!!

OK! We were ready to make a plan.

"First up," said Isabel. "We should all go around and ask our friends what they think of INSPIRE."

OK!

"Then we need someone to find out all about INSPIRE," Isabel continued. "Who likes to do online stuff?"

ME! "I can do that!" I said.

"OK, Maddy on Internet research. What if we make a video?"

"I've got a video camcorder!" Claire said. "I could do that."

"I could do that with you," said Kacey. "I took movie-making at camp this summer!"

"OK, Claire and Kacey on video," said Isabel. "We also need costumes. Who wants to do costumes?"

"Isabel, I think that should be YOU," Claire said. "You're so fashionable! And you want to be a fashion designer, right?"

"OK," said Isabel. "Costumes are me."

"And OK, we need to have a performance. Any ideas?"

We talked. We talked. And, we talked some more.

And this is what we decided:

- ★ We're going to lip synch to *Looking Up*.
- ★ We'll each play one girl in the group.
- ★ Claire and Kacey are going to make up the dance routine.
- ★ We'll pump up the crowd for INSPIRE's music!

The three of them were all excited. I was like ...

Umm ... Lip synch? Dance? In front of an audience?

I am so not great at being in front of an audience. I mean, I'm the girl who:

- ★ Tried to be sick on dance recital day. (The thermometer by the light bulb thing. Mom didn't buy it, of course.)
- ★ Pretended to have laryngitis when my mom made me go to drama camp. (Mom didn't buy that either. Said I should still go ... and mime.)
- ★ Didn't make cheerleading. (I think because the audience and judges were like "get that girl off that stage!")
- ★ Got so nervous on a catazine shoot, that I fell and knocked everyone over.

So, um ... lip synching? Dancing? In front of an audience?

What are the chances of me doing that without screwing up?

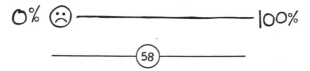

"Don't worry, Maddy," Isabel said. "We'll take it easy on your dancing. You can be Alexa. She sings and plays her guitar more than she dances, OK?"

OK. Yeah. I guess. That helps ... a little.

Eeeek!!!!

So we would all meet up again in two days. And we'd get ready for ...

TOO's U-PICK CHALLENGE CONTEST!!!!
TOO CREW VS. THE TALENT GIRLS

Woo Hoo!!!!

Lauren came back in the room. "Guess what, girls? I have a special treat for you. One of the singers from one of your groups is here in town and stopped by. I thought it would be nice for her to meet you and say hi." Lauren left.

Alexa! I bet it's Alexa! Because she's from here in Columbus, Ohio and all.

The door opened ... and in walked ...

The girl from POSE! The girl named Love!

Wow! Cool! Love was standing here in front of us!!!!! In true life! Wow!!! She was way pretty. Way glam. Like her hair was all long and wavy and shiny. She was wearing clothes that were, well, kinda rubbery. She had tons of makeup on. And sunglasses. Sunglasses? Inside?

"It's Love!" Sierra and Brittany both squealed. We all went over to her.

"Hi!" we said.

"So, I hear some of you are my fans?" Love asked.

"Ohmigosh," Brittany said, all gushy. "Did you hear that we totally want you to be *TOO's U-Pick Challenge* winner? Me and Piper and Sierra totally voted for you."

"I'm Sierra!" said Sierra, all mushy. "I voted for you!"

"Yes," Piper said, all cool. "Those girls over there voted for someone else. But we know that you guys deserve to win. POSE is totally hot."

"You have good taste," Love said to Piper. She looked over at me, Kacey, Isabel, and Claire.

And it was not a nice look. It was a SNOTTY look. Like you didn't vote for me? Um.

"Hello," said Claire. "I'm Claire, that's Kacey, Maddy, and Isabel. It's nice to meet you."

Love gave us a half-wave. Like, yeah whatever.

"Love, Love, could we get an autograph?" Brittany said.

"Oh, OK. I guess so," said Love. Like it was such a big hassle. Sierra gave her a pen.

To Sierra! One of my biggest fans!
Love from POSE!

To Brittany! One of my biggest fans!
Love from POSE!

Then she did ours.

To Maddy, Maybe you'll recognize talent someday.
Love

To Isabel, sorry you didn't choose better.
Love

To Kacey, maybe next time!
Love

To Claire, hope you change your mind.
Love

Oooooookay!!!!!!!

I looked at Kacey, Isabel, and Claire. We were all like ... Ouch!

Piper said, "Don't forget mine! Make it out to Piper. I'm so your biggest fan. I have to get an outfit like yours. It's just so fabulous."

Love signed an autograph for Piper.

Piper read it out loud. "To Piper, one of my biggest fans. And who has great taste. Love."

"Piper! That's so cool!" Brittany chirped.

Lauren came back in the room.

"I hope you guys have enjoyed meeting Love. But she has to get going."

"We singing stars have busy schedules!" Love said, all sweet-like, now that Lauren was here. "Buh bye!" She waved and blew a kiss. Mostly to Piper, Brittany, and Sierra.

"She is soooo COOL!" Sierra said. "So gorgeous!"

"Bet you guys are sorry you didn't vote for POSE now!" Brittany said to me.

Uh ... actually ... NO!

Because Love was ...

RUDE! ...

MEAN! ...

FAKE and PHONY!

I remembered how Alexa had been at the photo shoot.

Which was ... NICE!

Now, we really had to win! Because I wanted Alexa to win! I wanted INSPIRE to win! And also ... I have to say it ...

I didn't want Piper, Brittany and Sierra to win ... or Love.

Well, we've got our work cut out for us. We all better go get started!

✳ ✳ ✳ ✳ ✳ ✳ ✳

Search for: *INSPIRE music group*

Results: 72 matches

1st match: Music Group INSPIRE sings at charity event

New singing group INSPIRE says they want to do more than just sing and dance. "Like our name, we want to inspire people everywhere with our music!" says 14-year-old lead singer Alexa Chappell.

An appreciative audience was inspired by a charity performance INSPIRE did last night to raise funds to help animal shelters. Members of INSPIRE volunteer their time to help raise awareness for the dogs and cats available for adoption.

"I adopted my own dog, Rocky, from a pound," says Alexa. "So this was an event I really wanted to help with!"

INSPIRE's debut song, *Looking Up,* hit the airwaves this week.

I spent all afternoon on the computer. My dad helped me look up stuff on INSPIRE. I found out they became a group last year. They were all 14 and 15-year olds, and best friends from music camp. They were into singing, dancing and playing their instruments. They named themselves INSPIRE because they wanted to inspire girls to reach their dreams. They loved animals, beaches, and email. And their fans!

I liked everything I read about them!!!!

I did a little research on POSE, too. Their lead singer, Love, said they were all about looking good on stage. "If you don't look hot, what's the point?" was her big saying.

So, OK! Now I felt really good about choosing INSPIRE!

"You've worked very hard, Maddy," my dad told me. "Good job!"

I had! I had worked hard! And I had more work to do! I also was going to play the song to some of my friends. And find out what they liked about it. It's sorta like what Lauren called a focus group.

Lauren told me that a focus group is like when a business gets people together. To find out what they think about something.

Like you could do a focus group on a new kind of potato chip and have people taste it. And ask if they like them! Or not!

You could do a focus group for new sneakers and have people try them on. And find out if they look good! If they're comfy.

Or you could do a focus group on a new music group! And play their songs. And ask people what they like or don't like about it!

I was going to do my own focus groups. I was going to ask my friends and other kids about INSPIRE. At school. Yup. School. Which was starting ... TOMORROW!!!!

OHMIGOSH, SCHOOL STARTS TOMORROW!!!! YIKES!

I was way nervous all over again. Almost freaking out! Because the first day of school, you know? At a new school! New teachers! New lockers! (9-left, 19-right, 7-left! OK! Had my combination memorized! Whew!)

With half of it all new people. People I didn't know!

With nobody I knew in my lunch!

And nobody I knew on the afternoon bus! Ack!

Brittany had called me about it. "Maddy! Are you freaking out about school tomorrow? I'm dying to know who's in my classes! At least I don't have to worry about what to wear the first day. I'm sooo glad the cheerleaders get to wear our uniforms the first day! Aren't you totally stressing out about what to wear tomorrow?

I mean pressure ... the FIRST DAY OF SCHOOL OUTFIT!"

Um, yes. Thanks for putting it that way. I WAS stressing about it! Last year it was like this. We all were running over to each other's houses. Figuring out our outfits together. Taylor and Brittany and Haley and Danielle and me.

This year ... all those new people! Who have never seen me before. They'll be like "Who are you?!" And, "Do I want to be friends with you, yes or no??!!"

And my friends weren't helping! Their first day of school outfits were CHEERLEADING UNIFORMS! And mine wasn't.

Should I wear:

- ★ Blue shirt
- ★ Denim skirt
- ★ Gold hoop earrings
- ★ Lucky choker

Or:

- ★ White shirt
- ★ Olive Vest
- ★ Olive-ish pants
- ★ Round silver earrings
- ★ Lucky choker

Or maybe:

- ⭐ Denim shirt
- ⭐ Khaki skirt
- ⭐ Gold and blue earrings
- ⭐ Lucky choker

Or ...

AUGH!!!!!

OK. I have to say this. I was nervous about EVERYTHING! I was trying not to feel sad, too! And bummed out! But school was looking like it was going to be pretty lonely this year.

And oh. Speaking of sad. And bummed out. And lonely. I had something else to do tonight ...

Dogsitting. Time to take care of Scrumptious.

I got Miss Phipp's house key. I went over to her house. To see cute, little Scrumptious. Sad, bummed out little Scrumptious.

I only had two days left before Miss Phipp came home. And I was still ... The World's Worst Dogsitter.

I am serious! But I couldn't give up. That poor little dog. So lonely! So sad! I had to keep trying to make her happy.

I opened the door to her house. I went to her pink little satin bed. Yes. There was Scrumptious. Lying with her little furry chin on her paws.

"Hi, Scrumptious!" I said. I sat down to pet her. "Hi, you cute little puppy wuppy. I'm here! I'm here to see you!"

She opened one eye to peek at me. Then she went SIGH! And closed her eye again.

Poor, poor Scrumptious.

I tried her doggie treat. Nothing. I tried her doggie toys. Nothing.

KNOCK! KNOCK! KNOCK!

Someone was at the door! I knew not to open the door. It wasn't my house. And I was alone in it! It could be some stranger!

"HEY MADDY! HEY! OPEN UP!"

Oh. It wasn't some stranger.

Just someone STRANGE.

My brother, Zack. I got up and opened the door.

"What do you want," I asked him. "Because I'm working. At

my job, here."

"Looks like you should be fired," Zack said. "Because that dog is looking real SAD, dude."

Gee, really? Thanks for pointing that out.

"Get out," I said.

"OK," Zack said. "I could help you out, you know."

"No thanks, no way," I said.

"Dad says to come home in 15 minutes," Zack said. "Since you have school tomorrow and all. And oh, Brittany called and left a message. Something like all the cheerleaders won't be on the bus tomorrow morning. Because they are going to school early to set up their candy sale."

AUGH! I don't even have anyone to sit with on the bus to school?!

I flopped down next to Scrumptious' pink satin bed.

"Move over," I told her. "We can be bummed out together."

I patted Scrumptious's soft white fur. I scritched her little ears. I smooched her little nose. She might be sad, but she was still super cute.

Then I heard the front door open again. It was Zack again.

"I've come to save your job!" he announced. "I know how to get that dog moving!"

Zack walked in the room. "Lookie what I found!" In his arms was ...

A cat!

The brown striped cat that runs around our neighborhood!

"Oh no!" I yelled. "Don't bring a cat in here!!!!!!!!!!!"

"MRRRRRRRRRRRRRRRROW!!!!!!!!"

Uh, oh ... too late!

The cat saw Scrumptious. And FREAKED! It started kicking its hind legs! It started scratching at Zack! It was trying to escape. "Hold on to it, Zack! Don't let it –"

"Ow!" Zack said, dropping the cat. "Stupid thing scratched me!"

"MRRRRRROWWWWWWWWWWW!" The cat was on the loose!

"Catch the cat, Zack!" I yelled. I jumped up.

The cat was in the kitchen! No wait! In the living room! No wait! In the dining room!

SCREEEEEEEECH! Oh no! The cat was climbing the curtains! Like using its claws and going scratch! Scratch! Scratching its way up.

Up!

Up!

To the top of the curtains!

Like it was SpiderCat or something!!!

"Zack! Get that cat!" The cat was spazzing out!!!! It jumped off the curtains like in a FLYING LEAP! Like it was SuperCat or something!!!

"Chase it! Chase it out the door!" I yelled. I ran to the left! Zack ran to the right!

The cat ran ... out the door!

WHEW!

Zack looked at me. I looked at Zack. We both looked at Scrumptious. She was peeking out of one eye at us. She hadn't moved. That whole entire time. She was still flumped out on her bed. She did one of her SIGH's.

"Looks like you're getting fired!" Zack said, cheerfully. "Been fun! But gotta run!"

And he ran out the door.

"You better run, Zack!" I yelled after him. "Fast and far, far away!"

ARGH!!!!!!!!!!!!!!!!!

chapter 7

Lunch time. Lunch is a good thing, right? I mean, food is good for you. You need food to live. You need to eat lunch. Lunch is nutritious. Lunch was pizza today. I liked pizza.

OK, WRONG! I WAS FREAKING OUT!! I was carrying my lunch tray. La la la. Walking to the tables. Not having anywhere to sit. Not having ANY OF MY FRIENDS IN 3RD PERIOD LUNCH!

Was it going to be true? Was I going to be a lunch loser? At a table all by myself? All alone?

Like on the bus this morning. Ugh. I got on and had nobody to sit with. Nobody! I sat by myself! I ducked my head so nobody would see me alone.

And now ... I'm alone again!

I looked around the cafeteria. Yeah, there were some people I knew. But they weren't my friends! So I couldn't be like, "Hi I am not your friend but can I sit here?" They would be like "LOSER! Go away!" I'm sure.

I had a plan. I would stand here for about 10 seconds. Pretending to be looking for somebody. Like, "Oh friends who are saving me a seat, where are you?" Because I have many friends to sit with, and I just need to spot them!

After that, I would bolt. Today, I'd hit the girl's room. Yeah, spending 45 minutes in the girl's room = no fun. But better than being a LUNCH LOSER. Tomorrow, I'd try the nurse's office. Lay on a cot for 3rd period. The next day ... I don't know! I'd have to think of something!!!!

10 seconds was almost up. 7 ... 8 ... 9 ... Girl's Room here I come ....

"Maddy! Hey, Maddy Sparks!"

Was I dreaming? Did I hear my name?

YES! Someone was calling my name.

I looked and saw a girl with black hair waving at me. It was Jordan Cooper! Jordan Cooper was sitting at a table, with a couple other girls. She waved at me. Jordan Cooper! She went to my old school with me! I knew her kind of. But not so much. Because Brittany didn't like her. She always said Jordan thought she was "all that." Brittany was even psyched when Jordan didn't make cheerleading.

But right now, I didn't care! Because she said ...

"Come sit with us!"

Wheeeeeew!

So I went. And sat down.

"Hi," I said. Kinda feeling stupid. 'Cuz I didn't really know these girls.

"This is Maddy," Jordan said. "And that's Petie."

"Hi!" said Petie. She had wavy-ish brown hair. She was wearing a blue hoodie and corduroys. She was smiling and looked nice.

"And that's Sara," Jordan said. Sara had wavy blond hair. She was wearing a long-sleeve white t-shirt with a cool letter S on it.

"Sara and Petie went to the other school," Jordan told me. "But I know them from dive team."

Hi! Hi! Hi!

We all said hi.

"How are your classes so far?" Jordan asked me.

"OK," I said. "The worst is coming this afternoon though. Seventh period. Choir!"

"I'm taking choir, too!" said Petie. "I like to sing, though. You don't?"

"I'm a way bad singer," I said. "I'm gonna flunk!"

I just knew it! I was going to bomb out of choir!

"It would be pretty cool to be a singer," said Sara. "Like in music videos and stuff."

Oh! Music videos! I could do my focus group! I needed more people to listen to INSPIRE. And tell me what they thought. So maybe I could ask Jordan, Petie, and Sara?

They wouldn't think it was too stupid, would they? I don't want to be all braggy. Like I get to do this cool TOO Crew stuff and ha, ha you don't. But they might think it's fun, right? To get to help out, too?

"Hey, um" I asked. "I have to do this thing? Like find out if you like this music or not. Um, do you guys want to listen to a couple songs? And tell me what you think?"

"Yeah! Sure!" they all said.

I got out a little video camcorder Claire had let me borrow. She had one that fit in my backpack. So I could tape what people said about INSPIRE. I opened it carefully. I didn't want to bust it or anything.

Then I pulled out my portable CD player and turned on *Looking Up*.

"That song's awesome!" Jordan said.

"I love that!" Petie said. "It makes me feel like dancing or something!"

"I like the words. Like when they said 'It's time for me to see, exactly what is real.' That's really cool," Sara said.

"Yeah. A fun song!" Jordan said.

I videotaped everything they told me. Yup, things are definitely looking up!

"Hey, girls. Any room for us?" It was Derek! Derek who lived on my street. Jordan moved over to make some room for Derek. And also for the guy following Derek. Who was ...

RYAN MOORE!

RYAN MOORE WAS IN 3rd PERIOD LUNCH!!

RYAN MOORE WAS SITTING DOWN AT MY LUNCH TABLE!!!

OK that was crazy. Because I mean, RYAN MOORE!

Yes! #1 on my Ultimate Crush List was Ryan Moore!

Dark brown hair. Deep blue eyes. And way cute.

And sitting across the table from me.

"So what classes do you guys have?" Jordan asked Derek and Ryan. They all pulled out their schedules. And started talking.

And I was like ...

NOTHING! I was saying NOTHING!

At least I wasn't saying GAH! Or Glak!

But NOTHING was not good either.

I just sat there. While everyone else was all like "You're in my language arts-social studies-band-math blah blah blah."

But wait! I remembered. I had a plan.

Yes. I had a plan. I knew I would see Ryan Moore, #1 on my Crush List at school. I had wanted to be ready! So I'd come up with a plan.

I was going to be like la la la. No big deal. And ask, "How was your summer?" And then he would say, "Good how was yours." And I would say all cool-like, "Great, thanks!"

That was the plan.

OK. Time for the plan.

Here goes.

I'm gonna do it.

"Um," I said. "Um."

Go Maddy, go! You can do it!

"Um, Ryan. How was your summer?"

"Good! It was really good!," he answered. "I went to my cousin's. I learned how to play guitar."

"Yeah!" Derek said. "We're going to put together a band. We're gonna ROCK!"

"A band?" Petie said. "How cool!"

"What kind of band?" I asked.

Good! I asked Ryan Moore a question. And it wasn't a dumb question! Good one, Maddy. Yessss!

"Rock," Ryan said. "Derek's on drums, I'm on guitar. Brandon Nash is our singer."

"That's cool you play your own instruments," I said. I thought of INSPIRE. And how cool it was the girls played their own music. It's hard to play an instrument!

"Do you play anything?" Ryan asked me. "Are you taking band or orchestra?"

"No," I said. "I'm going to be in choir. But I love to listen to music."

"That's cool," he said.

BRRAAAAAAAAAAAAAAAAAAAAAAANG!

The bell was ringing! Third period lunch was over! I had to go to ... um ... Social Studies next.

"Later!" Ryan Moore said. "See ya at lunch tomorrow, Maddy."

UM! Hel-lo?

Did Ryan Moore just say "See ya at lunch tomorrow?" To me?

SEE YA AT LUNCH TOMORROW! He definitely said it to me, right? I mean, he said "Maddy!" I'm the only Maddy! See ya tomorrow at lunch!!!!

AHHHHHHHHHHHHHH!!!!!!!!

This Journal Belongs to:

Maddy Elizabeth Sparks

Hello from 6th period Study Hall! I have nothing to study yet! Since it's still the first day. And I have no homework! Yay!!

I worked on my INSPIRE stuff. I got it all done! Whew! Tons of research. Tons of work! But I hope they win TOO's U-Pick Challenge. I want them to win really, really, really bad!

I got all my stuff ready! Kacey, Isabel, and Claire are going to come over after dinner tonight. To my house! My parents said OK. So we could practice for TOO's U-Pick Challenge Contest on Saturday!!!!

Yay! OK. I'm bored. Lalala. Nothing to do.

the TOO Crew!!

M usic lover	**K** ind
A wesome	**A** thlete
D og lover	**C** ute
D etermined	**E** nergy
Y ay for me!	**Y** ay for Kacey!

I nto fashion	**C** lassy
S tylin'	**L** oves horses
A dvice giver	**A** lways nice manners
B eautiful hair	**I** nteresting
E xcellent dancer	**R** eaaaaallly pretty
L ikes helping people	**E** asy to talk to

OK! That took up 10 minutes. 20 minutes left in study hall.

Here's my day:

1st - Math
who do I know - Haley, Surya

rating (1 to 10) - 5 Too early in the morning! But teacher kinda funny! Told some jokes.

2nd - Science
who do I know - Danielle, Shana, Chelsea B.

rating (1 to 10) - 7 Danielle is my lab partner!

3rd - Lunch
who do I know - Jordan Cooper, new girls Petie and Sara, Derek and RYAN MOORE!!!!!!!!

rating (1 to 10) - 10+++++++

4th - Social Studies

who do I know - Haley, Amanda

rating (1 to 10) - 4 Teacher is like ZZZZZ BO-ring
      I'm lost already.

5th - Language Arts

who do I know - Caroline, Quinn, Sara from lunch

rating (1 to 10) - 8 We wrote journals!

6th - Study Hall or Spanish

who do I know - Danielle, Derek

rating (1 to 10) - 7 Not allowed to talk. But me and
      Danielle are passing notes!!!!

7th - Choir or Wellness

who do I know - Brittany, Petie from lunch.

rating (1 to 10) - Probably a 0! 'Cuz that will be my
      grade! When they hear how I sing!!!!

So yes! I SURVIVED LUNCH!

I still have to survive choir. I still have to survive the bus ride home. BUT I DID SURVIVE LUNCH!

OK, and not just survived! Talked to Ryan Moore!!!! And HE TALKED BACK TO ME!!! Yes, it's true. I kept replaying it in my mind. This is what he said:

"Good! It was really good."

"I went to my cousin's. I learned how to play guitar."

"Derek's on drums, I'm on guitar, Brandon sings."

"Do you play anything?"

"Are you taking band or orchestra?"

"Cool."

and ... and ... AND ... the most important part ...

"See ya at lunch tomorrow, Maddy."

!!!!!!!!!!!!!!!!!!!!!!!

Danielle's passing me a note. G2G. More later.

To MAddy!

I'm SOOOO BORED! Fill this out And write me bAck!

How's school?

- [ ] Off to A pretty good stArt
- [ ] AWESOME!
- [ ] Not bAd
- [ ] The totAl Worst!

If you asked me last night I would have checked ☑ the total worst!

But now I checked ☑ off to a pretty good start!

Specially 'cuz of lunch! Now, if I can just survive choir ....

chapter 8

WHEN: Later that night
WHERE: At my house
WHAT: Getting ready for the TOO Crew to come over!

OK! Today's the day Kacey, Isabel, and Claire were coming over to my house! To practice our lip synch routine.

OK! OK then! OK why was I so nervous?

I mean, the TOO Crew are totally my friends now, right? Nothing to be nervous about! I hope they like my snacks. I hope they like my room. I hope they think my house is OK.

I mean, I didn't know what kind of houses they lived in. I'd never been to Kacey's house! Or Isabel's house! Or Claire's house!

Claire! Her house is probably some huge mansion! Her father was this major business guy. She might come to my house and go, "Oh."

No pool? No hot tub? No giant closets? No entertainment room with big flat-screen TV?

And be like, "Yuk! What a lame house!"

But OK. Claire was so nice. She wouldn't think like that.

Would she? Would they? Was it a mistake to invite them over?

I started pouring some snacks into bowls. One chips, plain. One fish crackers, extra cheesy. One kettle corn.

"Oh YEAH! Snacks!" Zack came in, carrying his skateboard. He headed to the bowl of chips.

"Get your hands off those snacks!" I growled. Then yelled. "MOOOOOOM! Zack's trying to eat all my snacks!"

"Zack!" my mom came in. "I thought you were going to be at Adam's house."

"Yeah, well," Zack said. "Adam's mom said she had a headache. And that I was the one giving it to her. Like what's that all about? Geez. So anyway I had to come home."

"Mom!" I said. "You promised Zack wouldn't be here when the TOO Crew got here!"

"Sorry, Maddy," my mom said. "I tried. I'll keep him out of the way. Zack won't bother you."

Yeah, right! Like that's ever been true in my entire life!

BRRRRRING!

Doorbell! They're here!

I opened the door. Kacey, Isabel, and Claire were here! Kacey's mom had driven them. So my mom and her mom started talking about how school's starting and isn't that great, and blah blah blah.

I don't know why. It was kinda WEIRD to see the TOO Crew in my living room.

"Come on up to my room!" I said. "My mom's going to bring up snacks." We went upstairs.

"Your mom is sooo nice," Claire said. "She was really nice when we went to Hollywood."

"Yeah, she was cool," Isabel said.

We went into my room.

"Oooh, I like your room, Maddy!" Kacey said, dancing around my room a little. "It's so you!"

I liked it! It was blue! My favorite color. I wanted it to look like the beach. I had a blue comforter with this white net coming down over my bed. With white curtains, and white and blue tie-dye pillows. I had my shell collection with one of those shells you hear the ocean inside.

"Hey, look," Kacey said. "There's that Brittany from the Talent Girls!"

She was looking at the pictures stuck on my bulletin board. Of me and my friends. Brittany, Haley, Danielle all laughing and stuff ....

"Is that Taylor?" Isabel asked, looking too. "With the braids?"

Yes! There was a big picture of me and Taylor, my BFF together. We were holding our Build-A-Bears. And we were smiling.

But not for long. 'Cuz she had to move the next day.

"Yeah," I said, all sad.

"She looks nice," said Claire. She gave me a little hug. She knew I missed Tay.

"And now, we should probably do our presentation," Isabel said.

I went over to my desk. I got out my folder with my research in it. And then ...

"Hello! I'm here!" Zack was kicking at my door. Bang! Bang!

AUGH! Nooooo!

"Zack," I said, trying to be polite. "Stop kicking at my door. And please leave us alone."

"But my hands are full," he said. "'Cuz I brought some hot food mom made," he said. He kicked the door open and busted in. He did have a tray with all the plates balanced on it.

I looked at Kacey. And Isabel and Claire. They knew what I had to deal with! They knew all about Zack!

Like that time he put the worm in my suitcase!!!

Ewwww. I was grossed out just thinking about that!!!!

But he DID have snacks. And they smelled good!

Mini pizzas! Cheese sticks! Yum! So ...

"Oh, all right."

"Hi, I'm Claire," said Claire. "Nice to meet you, Zack."

Isabel and Kacey introduced themselves, too.

Zack flopped down on my bed. "So! What are we talking about?!"

"Nothing, Zack. We are WORKING," I said. "So you need to go."

"OK. I will," he said. But he slid down to the floor. And lay down on his back. "But first, guess what I am?"

Oh NO! He started waving his arms and his legs in the air. And making dog whining noises. And acting all like a crazy dog!!!! Like I did trying cheer up Scrumptious!!!!

Zack is totally humiliating me! I AM SO EMBARRASSED!

"I know what you are!" Isabel said. "You're a beautiful butterfly, coming out of her cocoon."

"UGH!" Zack said. "No way! Listen!"

He made some dog noises.

"Oh! I know! I know!" Isabel said. "You're a sweet cute little baby boy, aww. That's soooo sweet, Zack!"

"NO WAY!" Zack said. "I'm NOT sweet! Look! See! I'm a freaking-out dog! That's what Maddy was doing this one day, acting like a freaking-out dog. Get it? She was doing all this weird stuff! See? I'm all weird and freaky!"

"No, no, you're not," Isabel said. With a totally straight face. "You're definitely a cute little baby. I think it's so adorable. I want to huggle and cuddle you."

She held out her arms.

"AUGH!" Zack yelped. And he jumped up. "Don't come near me." And he ran out of the room!

NIIIIIIIICE!

"Isabel!" I said. "That was awesome! You totally faced him!"

"I babysit a lot," Isabel said, all cool. "I'm an expert."

Kacey gave her a high five.

"But wait," Isabel said quietly, putting her finger to her lips. "He's not totally gone."

Huh?

We all listened. Yes, I heard his footsteps. Quiet. Sneaky. Coming closer. Closer. Stopping by the door. Zack was totally spying on us!

"Yup, he's there," Isabel whispered. Then she said in a way loud voice, "Maddy! Your brother Zack is soooo sweet!"

"Yeah," Kacey said. Way loud, too. "Let's have him come back in. He can stay with us while we talk about girl stuff. Like nail polish and makeup."

"Yeah!" Isabel called out. "We can give Zack a makeover! He can be like a precious little doll for us to play with ...."

"BLEAH!!!" we heard from outside my door. And then footsteps. Fast footsteps. Going away. Far, far away.

"He's gone," Isabel determined.

High fives all around. Heh! See you later, Zack! Way later!

Buh-bye! Heh, heh.

Zack gone. Now ... time to work!

We plotted. We planned. We snacked, too. I showed them my research.

"So now I love INSPIRE even more! I mean, their song totally cheered me up. But they also help charities! And want to help girls!" I said.

"Maddy, I really think you should give the speech," Claire said. "You're so good at talking about INSPIRE. You can tell you are such a fan!"

"It's true, Maddy," said Kacey. "I mean we all like INSPIRE a lot. But you're so ... so totally inspired by them. I think the audience will be like, Wow! after you talk. Plus, you did so much research! You are like an expert on them, now!"

Me? Give the speech? In front of the audience?

"Um, I don't think so," I said. "I'll totally screw it up. I'll be so nervous! And completely ruin everything for INSPIRE!"

"Oh, all right," Isabel said. "I'll do the speech. But then Maddy has to take my part. The dance routine with the flip and split ...."

ACK!

"OK! OK! I'll do the speech!" I said.

And then ... it was time to learn the lip synch routine. I'd been memorizing all the words to *Looking Up*! It wasn't too hard though! Because I loved the song!

Things are looking up! Oh yeah! Things are looking up!

OK, here's the routine:

    ★ Maddy is Alexa, who sings the lead in *Looking Up*.
    ★ Kacey, Isabel, and Claire are the backup singers.

This is what Kacey, Isabel, and Claire have to do:

- ★ Step 1 and 2
- ★ Cross turn
- ★ Clap left twice and right turn
- ★ Step kick
- ★ Push back
- ★ Step 7 and 8

This is what I have to do:

- ★ Sing and jam out on the guitar.

OK! Yup! Better for me! Because like, "Wow!" Isabel, Kacey, and Claire totally nailed their routine in only ten minutes.

They were all like SUPER DANCERS!

And I'm like SUPER KLUTZ! It would have taken me three days! Or maybe even three years!

I was so lucky Alexa plays guitar. I could hide behind it and just kinda move around. Whew!

And that I didn't have to sing out loud, either!

Because I'm a way bad singer. I know I said that before. And everyone is supposed to say they're way bad at things. Even if you're not. So you don't act like you're all that or something.

But this time it's for real! My choir teacher confirmed it.

I had choir 7th period yesterday. We all sang for her. To see if we would be sopranos. Those are the high note singers. Or altos. Altos sing lower. Or bass. Those are really low singers.

I sang my notes for her.

Do! Re! Me! Fa! So! La! Ti! Doooooo!

And my teacher goes like this, "Well! Thank you, Maddy! That was a fine effort!"

Meaning, I tried hard. But I stunk. And then it got even worse!

Then she says, "Er, Maddy. I haven't gotten quite a handle on which category you are. So we will try again tomorrow. Try drinking some warm tea with lemon. That might help."

YOWCH!

Yup. So it's really a good thing I'm only lip synching at *TOO's U-Pick Challenge* Contest.

"OK, I think we've got it!" Isabel said to Kacey and Claire. She sat down on my bed. "Break time! Good job guys!"

"Yeah, you guys are awesome!" I said to them.

"You're pretty good yourself, Mad!" Kacey said.

Yeah, right. I rolled my eyes.

"I saw that," Isabel said. "Stop rolling your eyes. You were good. And you're NOT a bad dancer like you keep saying."

"Are you trying out for basketball cheerleading?" Claire asked.

Yipes! I couldn't even think about that yet! "Let me get through the first week of school first," I squeaked. "Snacks anybody?"

We snacked out. Munch! Crunch! Isabel was sitting on my bed. Kacey was lying on a pillow on my floor. Claire was sitting in my blue butterfly chair. And I was on my beanbag.

"How cool would it be to be in a band?" Isabel asked.

"If I were in a band, I'd call it the Sporties!" Kacey said. "And everybody in it would wear a different kind of uniform! I'd wear a soccer one. No wait, basketball! No, wait a softball one!"

I could totally see that! I could see Kacey bouncing all over the stage in a band.

"My group would be hip hop," said Isabel. "I think I'd call

myself Miz Is. Yeah ... it'd be cool."

"My band would be ..." Claire thought for a second. "No, I'd be just a plain singer. Like me and my piano."

I'd be in a band! And I would be the singer (hey, it's MY fantasy, OK?) My backup group members would be Austin Hamilton on drums. Aaron Carter would sing, too. Like duets with me. Hee. And ...

Ryan Moore on guitar.

Yeah. That would be an awesome band. Oh yeah.

I would write the lyrics. They would be like ... um ...

Yeah! We're in this together!
Yeah! Always and forever!

OK, I need to work on the lyrics.

"Maddy! Earth to Maddy!"

Oh! I'd been spacing out!

Then OOF! A pillow swopped me in the face!

"HEY! Isabel!"

"Just trying to snap you out of it, space girl," Isabel said, smiling.

"Oh yeah?!" I said. I grabbed my blue tie dye pillow off my bed.

And threw it right back at her. SWOP!

"PILLOW FIGHT!" Kacey yelled. "You guys are doomed! I'm the master of pillow fights!"

"Not likely!" Claire said. And she reached over and pulled out the pillow Kacey was sitting on! And whomped her over the head with it.

"Hey!" Kacey yelled, from the floor. "Claire's getting violent!"

BONK! Isabel tossed another pillow at Kacey!

I threw one at Isabel! Isabel clobbered me back!

Pillows were flying! Blue pillows! White pillows! Pillows were everywhere!

We were out of control.

"OK! OK! Enough!" said Claire, resting her head on a couple pillows. "I'm exhausted!"

We all put our pillows down.

"PSYCH!" Claire yelled. And she threw those pillows at us! Oof! She got me in the face! Bonk! She got Isabel! And then Kacey, who got hit so hard she went down!

"Claire! You totally tricked us!" Isabel said all pretend shocked. "You're SNEAKY!"

We were CRACKING UP!

Then, "Knock, knock!" I thought I heard a knock.

"Maddy, I think someone's knocking at your door," Claire said. I went over and opened it.

It was Zack.

"WHAT?!" I demanded.

"Mom says don't forget you have to dogsit," Zack said all fast and rushed.

"Oh! It's Zacky!" Isabel called out to him. "Come on in! Precious little boy!"

Zack turned all red. And totally took off down the hall.

"Isabel," I said to Isabel. "You are GOOD."

"I'll have to remember that trick!" said Kacey. "In case I have a little brother. Who tries to cause trouble!"

Could happen! 'Cuz Kacey's mom was pregnant. Waaaaaaaay pregnant. Kacey already had a little sister, Emily, who was a cutie pie. Kacey got to pick the baby's name herself!

Babies are sooooo cute!!!! I mean, even Zack was cute when he was a baby! Until he turned into ... Zack. Blugh.

"Hey, guys," I said. "I have to dogsit. If you want to wait here for me, that's OK."

"Do you want us to come with you?" Claire asked. "I love dogs!"

OK! Um. But if they came with me, I'd have to tell them something.

"Well. Um. OK. The thing is," I confessed. "Dogsitting isn't going so great. I mean, this dog? Scrumptious? She's really cute. And when I first met her she was happy and friendly. But when I dogsit her, she's ... sad. Seriously sad. Way bummed out."

"Oh, poor puppy," Claire said.

"And poor you!" Isabel said. "Let's see if we can help out with this sitch. Come on! We're on a TOO Crew mission! To cheer up Scrumptious!"

chapter 9

"Oh," Claire said. "You're right, Maddy. That is a sad, sad dog."

Kacey, Isabel, Claire and I were sitting on the floor of Miss Phipp's kitchen. Looking at Scrumptious. Scrumptious was lying there. But hardly noticing us. She had her eyes closed.

"Yeah," I said. "My mom checked on her this morning. To make sure she wasn't sick or anything. Miss Phipp comes back tomorrow."

Whew! Hang in there, Scrumptious!

"Poor, poor little Scrumptious," Kacey said. "Maybe she wants to play! Maybe she likes to play ball? I think I've got one! We can try it!"

Kacey reached into her backpack. She pulled out a tennis ball. Then she pulled out a rubber ball. Then she pulled out a super bouncer ball.

"Do you have a basketball in there, too?" Isabel asked her, smiling.

"Oh! Not today! I have to have my BIGGER backpack for that!" Kacey said, scrunging around in her backpack. "But I do have a softball in here somewhere, too."

"Kacey!" we were all CRACKING up!

"Try the tennis ball," Isabel suggested.

Kacey rolled it to Scrumptious.

Scrumptious didn't even look up.

"Come on, Scrumptious! Wanna play ball?! Doggies love ball!" Kacey tried. She rolled the rubber ball to Scrumptious.

BOINK!

It boinked Scrumptious on the nose.

"Ooops! Sorry, Scrumptious!" Kacey said.

Scrumptious opened one eye. Put her chin on her paws. And went ... sigh.

"How about a super bouncer, Scrumptious?" Kacey said. She bounced it.

WHOA! That was a super serious super bouncer! It bounced off the ceiling! It bounced back to the floor! It flew right at us!

"Take cover!" I yelled. "Crazy super bouncer ball!"

I ducked! Isabel jumped under the kitchen table. Claire hid her head under her arms!

The ball bounced around Scrumptious! BOINK! Boink! And finally slowed down. Bonk.

"Ooops!" Kacey giggled. "Sorry guys!"

We all looked at Scrumptious. She peeked back with one eye. It stayed open.

"Hey, one eye is looking," I said. "That's progress."

"Maybe it would cheer her up to hear Miss Phipp's voice. We could call Miss Phipp?" Claire suggested. "I have lots of free minutes left on my cell phone."

"Good idea, but can't," I said. "She's traveling home. I don't know where to call her."

We all sat down on the floor ... to think.

What could we do? This dog was so, so SAD!

"Poor Scrumptious," Claire said, petting the dog's head. "Did your mommy go on vacation and you didn't get to go? Is that why you're so sad?"

"That's it!" Isabel jumped up. "Scrumptious needs a vacation!"

Huh? "Um, I tried to take her for a walk around the block," I said. "It didn't go so well. So a vacation ...?"

"How about a doggie spa!" Isabel said. "We can pamper Scrumptious right here!"

"That's so crazy!" Kacey giggled.

"Well, I think she will love it," Claire said, seriously. "It would be a relaxing break from all of her stress and worries."

We all CRACKED up.

"What?" Claire asked. "That's what my father's girlfriend says when she goes to the spa."

"What does she do at the spa?" I asked Claire. I'd never been to a spa.

"Sometimes she gets a massage," said Claire, thinking. "And seaweed facials. And her hair done. Oh! And her nails done, too. She said she'd take me if I wanted. But the seaweed thing, I don't know. Sounds too gooey and gross."

OK! Let's do it!

"Welcome to the TOO Crew Doggie Spa, Scrumptious," I announced to her. "A FABulous and GLAMorous escape from all of your worries."

Scrumptious gave a sigh.

"We could start with a massage!" Kacey said. "Everybody, massage Scrumptious!"

Kacey petted her head! Isabel scritched her ears! Claire rubbed her belly!

I ... I ... wasn't sure what I was supposed to do.

"Um, what part am I supposed to do here?" I said. "There's not much dog left."

"My father's girlfriend likes to get a foot massage," Claire suggested. So I gave Scrumptious a paw massage!

Hm. And then ...

Scrumptious made a little noise. Like this, "werf!"

"A noise!" I said. "A noise! Scrumptious made a noise! She hasn't said anything! Except sigh! What do you think werf means? It sounded good! Do you think it's good?"

I was so excited! Scrumptious made a noise!

"Let's keep giving her the spa treatment!" Kacey said. "Maybe it's working!"

"What's after massage?" Claire asked.

"How about hair!" Kacey said. "Or, I guess, fur!"

"I have the hair supplies," Isabel said, opening her bag. "I have a new brush and new hair bands to contribute."

We brushed! We fluffed!

Isabel did Scrumptious' fur in little bands. She pulled her hair out of her eyes. She made little puppy tails. A little piggytail for each side of her head.

Awwwwww! "Scrumptious, you look sooooo cute!" I told her.

Scrumptious opened both eyes. And lifted her head off her paws. Maybe she WAS feeling better????!!!

"What else?" I asked. "Should we do her nails? How about a PET-i-cure?"

Get it? Like a pedicure? PET-i-cure? HA, HA?

OK. Anyway. Isabel shot a hair band at me for that bad joke.

"How about we have her go to wardrobe?" Kacey said. "Like we did at the catazine shoot."

"Perfect," Isabel said. "Jazz up her look. Scrumptious, we'll get you all stylin!" Isabel pulled the bandanna off her head. And wrapped it around Scrumptious' neck. Ta da!

The new, improved Scrumptious!!! Fluffy and shiny! And all kinds of cute with those puppytails!

And OK! She was looking at us. Her head was up.

"Well," I said. "She looks better. But not like Woo Hoo! Happy Dog!"

"Bruno's coming to get me in about 20 minutes," said Claire, checking the time on her cell. "We could think more about how to cheer up Scrumptious? And maybe rehearse our routine one more time?"

"Sure," I said. I turned on the CD player we'd brought over with us from my house and hit "2."

We all lined up like we'd practiced. Ready ...

Today is my day, to change how I feel.
It's time for me to see, exactly what is real.

Kacey, Isabel, and Claire did their moves!

I pretended to play my guitar and sing.

Things are looking up! Yeah! Things are looking up!

"WERF!"

Things are LOOKING UP! YEAH!!

"WERF! WERF! WERF!"

Kacey, Isabel, and Claire stopped dancing. I stopped lip synching. Because Scrumptious ...

Was barking. Like this, "WERF! WERF!"

And Scrumptious ...

Was getting up! And starting to move! And walking across the floor! And going ...

"WERF! WERF!"

We were all like, "What is it, Scrumptious? What is it, Girl?" Scrumptious went over and licked the CD player!

"I think she likes the music," Claire said.

"Maybe she's a fan of INSPIRE!" Kacey said.

"I know! I know!" I said. "It's like when I was all bummed out! And *Looking Up* was on and I felt better! It cheered ME up! Maybe it's cheering Scrumptious up!"

OK that was kinda weird! But Scrumptious HAD been sad and lonely like me! So maybe INSPIRE cheered her up, too?!!!!

Yes, Scrumptious was wagging her tail! She was saying WERF and not SIGH! Her eyes were open. And she was looking at me. I think she was smiling! I am way serious! A cute little doggie smile! YAY!!!!!!

Happiness comes, and happiness goes.
But today is the day, my happiness grows.
Things are looking up! Yeah! Things are looking up!

We all started dancing around Scrumptious. I picked her up! And started dancing around with her. She seemed to like it!!

And then ... SCRUMPTIOUS LICKED ME! SHE GAVE ME A KISS! YAY!!!!!! YAY SCRUMPTIOUS!!!

"Woo Hoo!" We all screamed! "Yay Scrumptious!"

Things ARE looking up!!!!

chapter 10

Dling!

You have an Instant Message from BrittanyCheer! Will you accept?

Yes

BrittanyCheer:	Hi Maddy! U there?
MaddyBlue:	Hi!
BrittanyCheer:	Sup?
MaddyBlue:	I M online doing research. For TOO's U—Pick Challenge! I'm tired! Working on it all day!
BrittanyCheer:	LOL! Sorry 4 u! 'Cuz I was at the pool alllll day!
MaddyBlue:	Really?
BrittanyCheer:	Yup. Piper had the BEST idea and we didn't have to do ANYTHING!
MaddyBlue:	Serious?
BrittanyCheer:	Yeah. We spent like 2 minutes on it. While you were working all day! HA! Ours is AWESOME. Talent Girls ROCK!
MaddyBlue:	g2g dad is calling
BrittanyCheer:	TTFN! C U in choir!

My dad really was calling me. That wasn't an excuse!

OK! It's true! Sometimes I do make an excuse to get away from Brittany!!!

"Maddy," my dad said. "Your mom told me dogsitting went well for you today."

"Yeah! Scrumptious was so happy today!" I said. I hadn't told him about any of the ... not so good times! I wanted him to think I could handle it. So maybe ... maybe ... he would say yes we could get a dog!

"So!" I inched my way backward. "Is that all? Yup, it was great tonight. I'm going to go upstairs ..."

"Your mom also told me some other days didn't go so well?" dad interrupted me.

Snagged. "Yeah, Scrumptious wasn't happy," I confessed. "I tried everything!"

"And you kept trying, right?" dad said. "And didn't give up? Like I always say, Never give up!"

"Yeah. I kept going back. And then tonight we finally did it! We made Scrumptious happy!" I told him.

"Like I always say, hard work pays off," dad said.

"So, um ..." That's good! I'm thinking now's the time! To ask the Big Question. OK, I ask this Big Question everyday ... can I get a dog?

But now's the really right time ... OK, here goes ...

BEEP! BEEP!

"My pager," dad said, checking his pager. "Welp. Looks like it's time for me to do some work. I'm proud of your hard work, Maddy." He got up to go call the person back.

ARGH! Missed my chance. But ...

There would be other chances. I just knew it! Don't worry! I would ask again!

Iwantadog, Iwantadog, Iwantadog, Iwantadog, Iwantadog!!

OK. Anyway. I had more work to do, too! I needed to print out all the stuff on INSPIRE I'd found on the computer. I wanted to read it again so I knew it for sure. I wanted to practice my lip synch. I wanted ...

To be ready ...

For tomorrow ...

For ...

TOO's U-PICK CHALLENGE CONTEST!!!!

chapter 11

OK! So here I am! Walking into the mall. A different mall than I usually go to. But I'm here at this mall because ... this is where the CHALLENGE is going to be!

INSPIRE represented by the TOO Crew versus POSE represented by The Talent Girls!

Go INSPIRE Go! Go TOO CREW Go!

I'M WAY NERVOUS!!! Freaking out! But I'm trying to be calm ... stay cool ... keep it together.

I'm going to do it for INSPIRE! I believe in them!!!!!!

Mom, dad and Zack were with me. Mom was checking the mall directory to find out where we were supposed to go. I checked my backpack. It was heavy! Full of my CHALLENGE stuff:

★ Computer research stuff about INSPIRE
★ My speech
★ INSPIRE CD

And:

★ Lip gloss: The super shiny kind, tastes berry cherry

★ Disc Player: I listened to INSPIRE on it the whole way here! To pump me up!
★ My blue fuzzy journal
★ Two gel pens: Blue sparkle and green regular
★ Gum ... for after my speech
★ My book I'm in the middle of (it's way funny)

"OK, Limited Too is on the main level," mom announced.

We walked. Zack walked behind me. He was stepping on the backs of my shoes.

OW! I hate that!

"Zack," I hissed. "Stop it! Moooom, Daaaad, Zack's stepping!"

Mom gave Zack a warning look.

"What?" he asked all innocent.

"Zack," dad said. "Maddy has a big afternoon ahead of her. You are really not helping."

We kept walking.

"Hey, Maddy," Zack said.

"What?"

"Forget it," said Zack.

"Hey Maddy," said Zack.

"WHAT?!"

"Nothing," said Zack.

"Stop it! Why did we have to bring him here?" I whined.

"Good question," mom said. "I think I'll just find a pay phone and call Mrs. Hubert. She can come pick up Zack and babysit him for the rest of the day ...."

"ACK!" Zack yelled. "No Mrs. Hubert! When you guys were in Hollywood she made me eat beet pudding! She made me take a nap! OK, OK I'll be good Ma!!!!" Good one, mom.

We got closer to Limited Too. Lauren told us they were going to set up a little stage area for us outside the store.

There it was! There's the stage! Oh! The stage I'm going to be on. YIKES!

"Good luck, Maddy," mom said, giving me a big hug.

"You worked hard on this," dad said. "You'll be terrific." He gave me a hug, too.

"Yeah, wait," Zack said. "Here's my lucky rock."

"No way," I said. "That thing's going to explode or something! Nice try, Zack."

"Uh, no. It's just my lucky rock," he mumbled. And he stuffed it in my hand.

I looked carefully at it. It was really ... a rock. Oh! I guess he was really wishing me luck. Nice.

"Thanks, Zack," I said, trying to give him a hug.

"ACK! GROSS! Get her away from me!" he said. He ran ahead to mom and dad.

I followed them closer to the stage.

And there's Kacey! And Isabel! And Claire! They were all here!

THE TOO CREW WAS HERE!!

And they were wearing their INSPIRE clothes, too! Like me! This is what we were wearing:

- ★ Jeans - like INSPIRE did in their video!
- ★ Hats - like INSPIRE did in their video!
- ★ Our TOO Crew charm bracelets, of course!

And ...

★ T-shirts like INSPIRE did in their video!

Except ours were super special ... because Isabel designed our t-shirts. She used iron-on letters to put INSPIRE on each of them. Then she designed each one all different using some kinda paint that works on shirts. Mine was white and blue! With a little bit of sparkly. It was really cool.

"Maddy!" Isabel saw me. I ran over to them.

"Or should we say Alexa?!" Kacey squealed. "You look great!"

"So do you guys!" I told them. "Isabel, your shirts ROCK!"

"Thanks," said Isabel. She wanted to be a fashion designer when she grew up. Wow, she'd be great at it!

"Hi girls," Lauren came over to see us. "You look great. Let me take a picture of you!"

CLICK! ── the TOO Crew girls in their INSPIRE outfits!

Then she told us how it would work:

★ Lauren will announce us to the crowd.
★ The TOO Crew will give our presentation for INSPIRE.

★ The Talent Girls will give their presentation for POSE.

★ The audience will vote by yelling and raising their hands.

And either INSPIRE or POSE will be *TOO's U-Pick Challenge* Winners!!!!

In five minutes we would be on.

I stood with Kacey, Isabel, and Claire. OK. Now I was feeling super nervous. My stomach was like, whooomf.

I looked at my papers again. I'd practiced my speech a trillion times. I'd practiced my song a batrillion times. I'd been working really hard on this.

But now ... I wasn't so sure. I don't think I'm ready.

I thought of all the things so I'd be OK. I took deep breaths. In through my nose, out through my mouth. I thought of my favorite relaxing place. I even thought of another time I'd been nervous to go onstage. Monkey Girl, I thought. Hee. Monkey Girl WAS pretty funny.

I looked out at the crowd of girls starting to gather. I saw my mom, dad, and Zack. And Haley was here! She must have come with Brittany. Kacey's little sister, Emily. Hey, there was Jordan Cooper! And Petie and Sara. Cool.

All those people! I couldn't help it! Whoa, I was WAY nervous!

"Lauren," I whispered. "I feel sick. I'm thinking, um, maybe I can't do this."

"Maddy, you know this is normal. Even actors get nervous right before they go onstage," Lauren said.

"I know," I told her. "But this is well, more than like just about me doing a good job. It's not just me embarrassing myself. As usual. It's more. It's just ... I really love INSPIRE. I really want them to be the winners of *TOO's U-Pick Challenge* Contest. If I screw-up up there, I'll ruin it for them."

"Maddy, think about it," said Lauren. "You wouldn't be nervous if you didn't care about this. You care about INSPIRE. You really believe in what you're going to be saying, right?"

Yes! That's true!

"Then just remember how much you love INSPIRE's music," Lauren said. "And the audience will see it, too. And guess what?"

"It's time!"

chapter 12

It's TIME! Time to start!

TOO's U-PICK CHALLENGE CONTEST WAS GOING TO BEGIN!

Claire grabbed my hand. Kacey grabbed my other hand. Isabel was holding Kacey's hand. We looked at each other. We were ready!

Lauren was on stage giving the opening speech.

Lauren said, "Today, all of you girls will be making a choice. You will choose the music group who will perform at Toopalooza as *TOO's U-Pick Challenge* Contest winners. It's quite an honor. You'll choose between two new music groups, INSPIRE and POSE. We have two groups of girls who will be presenting their favorite to you. And then you will vote for the one you like best."

Woohoo! The audience was clapping! YEAH!

"First up ... The TOO Crew who is representing INSPIRE!"

OK. That was us! That was me! I was first! OK! Oh, Boy! Here I go!

I walked up the steps to the stage. Isabel, Kacey, and Claire followed me up.

My head was all buzzy. All fuzzy. My heart was pounding. My hands were sweaty.

It seemed like I was in a dream.

The crowd was quiet. The song was ending. OK. Here I go. Wish me luck.

I went up to the microphone.

"Hi ...." I started. "Um, I'm Maddy. And this is Kacey, Isabel, and Claire. There was this day. I was really bummed out. Feeling all alone. You know how it is. When you're just lying there going: Are things ever going to get better?"

I looked at the audience. Some of the girls were nodding. Yup. They'd been there, too.

"So, um, I turned on the radio. And there was this song I never heard before. And when I was listening to it, I all of a sudden started feeling better. The words cheered me up. The music pumped me up."

"And that song was by INSPIRE," I said. "And ever since, I've been like, I want all girls to be able to hear this song. Because even though yeah, it was just a song, it meant a lot to me."

"And I heard their other songs and loved them, too. And I

found out lots of things about them." And then I mentioned things about INSPIRE like:

- ☆ They play their own instruments.
- ☆ They practice together almost every day so they can get better and better.
- ☆ They do a lot of charity stuff, like at animal shelters.
- ☆ They want to inspire girls everywhere.

"So anyway, we're really into this new group INSPIRE. We think you might be, too. Once you find out a little more about them."

Claire clicked on a button. And music started playing ...

Thinking you're facing the world all alone?
It's all going by without you,
Thinking that things will never be good again?

And a video started on a big TV screen. Kacey and Claire had worked really hard on a video for today.

This is what was on it. First, INSPIRE singing *Looking Up!*

Then girls saying what they thought of INSPIRE.

- ☆ There was Petie: "I love that! It makes me feel like dancing or something!"
- ☆ And Sara: "I like the words. Like when they said, 'It's

time for me to see, exactly what is real!'"

★ And Isabel's friends, Nicole and Tia: "We love INSPIRE! They rock!"

★ And my friend Danielle: "This song makes me think of happy times!"

★ And Jordan Cooper: "Yeah. I just feel really good when I hear it!"

And some other girls. Then we had another video of INSPIRE singing another song called *True to You*. And then ...

The End!

Everyone clapped!!!!

OK I have to say this. It was an awesome video. We all worked really hard on it! And the audience was clapping!

We all got in our places. It was time for the lip synch!

"And now, we'd like to do our own performance of INSPIRE," Isabel announced. "The words will be on the screen. You can sing along if you want."

Looking Up by INSPIRE!

I played my guitar! Kacey, Isabel, and Claire did their dance!

You think you're alone, girl? Just listen to this song, girl!
And see that's all so wrong ... 'cuz ...
Things are looking up! Oh yeah! Things are looking up!

OK! I was rocking out! Jammin! Yeah! OK! OK oops! I did bump into the side of the stage. OK! But I'm OK! Keep going, Maddy ... keep lip synching ... keep air guitaring ... and ...

Happiness comes, and happiness goes.
But today is the day, my happiness grows.
Because things are LOOKING UP!
Yeah, things are looking up!

Things couldn't be looking any better!

And one ... two ... three ... DONE!

"Thanks, everybody!" we all yelled. And ran off the stage.

We did it! We did it!!!!!

WOO HOOOOOOOO!!!!!!!

Lauren walked by on the way up to the stage. "Nice work, girls," she said.

"We did it!" Kacey said. We were all like yay! We did it!!!!

But now, what were the Talent Girls going to do?

"Next up, the Talent Girls," Lauren announced. "Representing the music group, POSE."

Piper, Brittany, and Sierra went on the stage. They were wearing outfits like POSE; these really shiny tops and sparkly pants.

Everyone in the audience was like, Whoa. The outfits were um, very, very glittery.

"I'm Piper," Piper said into the microphone. "We want you to vote for POSE. POSE wears the most awesome clothes. They're all totally gorgeous. And guess what. Instead of me telling you about them, why don't you see it for yourselves?"

And all of a sudden, three girls in tube tops and sparkly pants ran on the stage. Wait a minute ....

"That's right," Piper said. "We don't need a video. HA! We brought you ... the real thing! Presenting ... POSE!!!!!"

Ohmigosh! The real POSE was here!

We were sunk!

"Hi girls," said Love, the lead singer. "We're POSE. We wouldn't usually do something like this. I mean, we sing at bigger places than the mall, OK? But, hey, they paid us lots of money for this. So here we are. OK girls, strike a pose!"

The girls struck a pose. And the music started. They started to sing. They started to dance.

And the audience was going ...

Crazy!!

I looked at Isabel, Kacey, and Claire. We were all like ...

Looking surprised. Shocked ... and bummed.

So anyway. I guess that was it. I really thought INSPIRE was better. That INSPIRE should win.

But how could we compete with THAT??!! Sorry, Alexa. We tried.

Brittany came bouncing over to me. "Are you like totally surprised, Maddy?" she asked me. "Can you BELIEVE we got the real POSE to come? Told you we'd blow you away!"

"How'd you get them to come?" I asked her.

"Oh, Piper's dad has connections. He flew POSE out here to do this. It cost big bucks. But he wanted Piper to win."

I tried to watch POSE sing. But Brittany kept talking and jumping around.

"So ha! We didn't do anything! You guys were doing all this work! And it was all for nothing! Ha! We Talent Girls Rule!"

And then ... Brittany was jumping around ...

And her foot got caught. On this extension cord. Which was plugged into the stage.

And then the music stopped. But POSE kept singing.

"Ohmigosh," Brittany said, trying to untangle the cord from her shiny pants.

Without the music, POSE sounded like ...

WAIIILLLLLL! YIYYYYYYYY!

Without the music, POSE sounded really weird. Like, their singing was really bad.

Just say that POSE sounded like they needed some hot tea with lemon ... and a LOT of it!

"Whoa," said Isabel. "They really can't sing! Sounds like POSE is fake!"

OHHHHHHHHH! The audience was gasping. Because I guess they were thinking that, too! They were whispering, "They can't sing! POSE can't sing!"

POSE realized what was going on. They looked around. They were looking ... WAY MAD!!!

Love, the lead singer gave Piper the biggest dirty look.

And then Love goes, "We should never have come to this stupid little mall thing."

Oops! Her microphone was on. So everybody heard her.

Love was not looking happy. And then POSE stormed off stage.

Yikes.

Lauren was on stage. She asked the audience to quiet down. And she called Piper, Brittany, and Sierra to come up. She gave Piper the microphone.

"Sorry, uh, just a little technical difficulty," Piper said, all sweet. "We're working on it."

"Well, so, we got to see a little of POSE's performance. Now why don't you tell us more about POSE," Lauren said to Piper.

"Well, did you see their outfits? Aren't they the cutest?" Piper said. "And Love? Isn't she soooo gorgeous."

She handed the microphone to Sierra. Who stood there frozen. And then Piper, Brittany, and Sierra just stood there. "Anything else?" Lauren asked. "Can you tell us a little about their background? Or what they are like?"

Piper, Brittany, and Sierra just stood there. Not saying a word. And then Piper shook her head. And goes, "No. Not really."

The audience was all whispering.

"Well, I guess that's it, then!" Lauren announced. "Looks like it's time to take a vote."

And OK! Time to vote!

Lauren asked everyone who wanted to vote for POSE to cheer and raise their hands. And it was like ...

Yay.

It was like Haley and two other girls.

Then Lauren asked who wanted to vote for INSPIRE. And this is what it was like YAY!!!!!!!

"Well, it sounds like the winner of *TOO's U-Pick Challenge* Contest is ... represented by the TOO Crew ... INSPIRE!" Lauren said.

WOO HOOO!! WOOOOOOO HOOOOOO!

Kacey, Isabel, Claire and I were jumping all over the place. "We did it! WE DID IT!!!!"

High-fives! Yays! The audience was cheering! And so was I! I WAS SO HAPPY!!!!!!!!!!!!!

Then I saw Piper and Sierra go over to Brittany. I overheard Piper say, "You RUINED everything, Brittany. I saw you pull that plug out. This is all your fault."

Brittany was like all red and stuff.

"I'm soooo sorry, Piper! It was an accident! And I didn't know POSE couldn't sing, I mean I didn't know they were fake ..."

"Oh, shut up, Brittany!" Piper said. "Come on, Sierra. Let's get out of here."

And Piper and Sierra took off. Leaving Brittany behind.

I felt sorta sorry for Brittany. Really.

chapter 13

The audience was starting to leave. My mom, dad, and Zack came over to me.

"Congratulations, honey!" mom said. "That was wonderful."

"Yeah! That was awesome! When the music went off! And those singers were like WAILLLLLLLL!" Zack started making this terrible noise. "And the audience was like Whoa! They can't sing! Heh heh, that was awesome."

"Now Zack, don't be happy about somebody else's misfortune," mom scolded him.

"Yeah, whatever, mom," Zack said. "Face it. They stunk!"

"Looks like all your hard work paid off," dad said to me. "You could tell the TOO Crew worked hard on this. You know, I've been awfully proud of you lately. First the dogsitting. Now this."

Yay!

OK! Now's my chance! To ask the Big Question!

"So ... um ... may we um ... " I asked. "Speaking of dogsitting ... can we ... can we ..."

OK, just ask!

"Can we get a dog?"

"Well you know I'm always impressed with hard work," dad said. "So ... let's just say I'll think about it."

THINK ABOUT IT! DAD SAID HE'LL THINK ABOUT IT!!!

He always says NO! No way! No how! Never!

But now ... he's thinking about it!!!!!

OK! OK! THIS IS GOOD! THIS IS ... REALLY GOOD!

"Maddy! Maddy!" Isabel, Kacey, and Claire were sitting on the stage with Lauren. They were all waving me to come over.

"We'll wait over here," said dad.

I went up on stage. It was a lot easier to be up here now! Without six trillion girls staring at me!

"Congratulations, TOO Crew," said Lauren. "You did a wonderful job representing INSPIRE."

It sure didn't seem like it for awhile! Like when POSE went up on stage I thought, No way! We lost for sure!

But we didn't! We won it for INSPIRE!!!!!!!!

Then ... Doo Deedle Doo Doo Doo!

Oh. Lauren's cell phone was ringing.

"Perfect timing," Lauren said, looking at her phone. "I have somebody on the phone who wants to talk to you."

???

Lauren held up her cell phone. And pressed a button.

"Hello," Lauren said. "You're on speakerphone. We can all hear you now."

"Hi Maddy! Hi Kacey! Hi Isabel! Hi Claire! It's Alexa!" the voice said.

Alexa from INSPIRE!

"All of us want to thank you," Alexa said. "We are sooo excited to be the winners of *TOO's U-Pick Challenge* Contest . We heard you guys did a great job."

"Thanks!" we all said.

"I knew when I met you at the catazine shoot I liked you

guys!" Alexa told us.

"Girls," Lauren said. "You put a lot of work into this presentation. And it showed. All of your hard work really made a difference. You really worked together, girls. You showed TRUE TEAMWORK. I think we could really use you girls at ... TOOPALOOZA."

What?!?!!!

"Yes," Lauren said. "We could use you at Toopalooza. To work behind the scenes. And then, see the concert. If you're interested of course."

INTERESTED? INTERESTED?!?!?!

I looked at Kacey, Isabel, and Claire. We all went ...

"AHHHHHHHHHHHH!!!!!!!! WE'RE GOING TO TOOPALOOZA!"

Ohmigosh. We were going to see:

- ☆ Aaron Carter!
- ☆ Jessica Simpson!
- ★ Mandy Moore!
- ☆ Nick Cannon!
- ☆ Play!
- ★ Ashlee Simpson!

And some newer groups like Nikki Cleary, Chantal Kreviazuk, and Jhene! And of course, INSPIRE!

YEAH! WE WERE GOING TO TOOPALOOZA!

"So I'll get to see you guys at Toopalooza!" Alexa said. "I can't wait!!!!"

ME TOO!!!! And ... oh! I thought of something.

"May I say something to Alexa?" I asked Lauren.

"Of course, Maddy!" Lauren said.

OK.

"I just wanted to tell you that I really love your music. And *Looking Up* really made me feel better this one day I heard it. So, um, thanks."

"Thanks! I love that song, too," Alexa said. And then she started singing.

And then Isabel started singing along, too. And then, Kacey. And then, Claire. And then ... even me!

Even with my voice. Because I knew even with MY voice, Kacey, Isabel, and Claire wanted me to sing with them!

Things are LOOKING UP! Yeah!
Things couldn't be looking any better!

SEE YOU AT TOOPALOOZA!!!!!!

Happy Face Rating:

 out of

the end ... for now that is!

Stay tuned to see what happens to the TOO Crew!

the too crew's
stuff for you to do

Make Your Band!

OK, remember when the TOO Crew made up their own bands?
My band members were Austin Hamilton, Aaron Carter ... and
Ryan Moore! I was the lead singer!

What kind of band would YOU be in??!!!

Band name:_____

Type of music:_____

Other members of the band:_____

Instruments:_____

Outfits:_____

You can write a song for your band, too! Go ahead, try it.

_____

_____

_____

_____

_____

_____

_____

Name Game

Do one of these for your name and for a friend! Like I did mine:

M usic lover   __ _____   __ _____

A wesome   __ _____   __ _____

D og lover   __ _____   __ _____

D etermined   __ _____   __ _____

Y ay for me!   __ _____   __ _____

                 __ _____   __ _____

                 __ _____   __ _____

                 __ _____   __ _____

School Chart!

How's YOUR school going? Rate your class periods like I did!
Rating 1 (lo) –10 (hi)

	Rating (1-10)	Why?
1st class period:	_____	_____
2nd class period:	_____	_____
3rd class period:	_____	_____
4th class period:	_____	_____
5th class period:	_____	_____
6th class period:	_____	_____
7th class period:	_____	_____

This Journal Belongs to:

Maddy Elizabeth Sparks

OK, bye! This is the end! But not forever of course!
Because we're going to Toopalooza next!

Toopalooza! A ginormous music fest! Famous singers!
Famous stars!

And me, Maddy Elizabeth Sparks! And of course ...
Kacey and Isabel and Claire!

You'll find out how it goes in ... **Tuned In Episode #4!**
Coming soon, exclusively to Limited TOO!

Maddy

G2G! TTYL! Byeeeeeeeeeeeeeeee!!!!!